AS WITCH WOULD HAVE IT

WICKED WITCHES OF PENDLE ISLAND BOOK 1

MARA WEBB

Pendle airport was a single strip of broken tarmac overgrown with weeds and long grass. A leaning radio tower turned around in the early morning mists while I stood outside a freezing shack that acted as the arrival and departure lounge. It was early and the sun was only just coming up, so it was still dark out, and it was still cold. Very cold.

The tin can airplane that had brought me here had been locked away in a crumbling hanger and its pilot, an older man by the name of *Smithy,* ambled back over to myself and the only other passenger from the flight. I imagined the airport had looked good once upon a time, but Smithy wasn't dressing down on account of the ageing facilities. He was wearing a full pilot's uniform and he obviously took pride in his job.

"I'd offer you a lift," Smithy said as he stuffed tobacco into his pipe. He used a match to light it and I worried his enormous white moustache was going to go up in flames. "But my car is already full. I take it you've both got a ride? There was a phone for a taxi, but the Pendle puma got to it."

Smithy nodded to the wall behind us, where three giant clawmarks had ripped an old payphone into shreds.

"Pendle… puma?" I said tentatively.

"Oh yes. She's been roaming this island for years. I saw her once. Giant beauty she is. Three hundred pounds of pure wildcat. There's a $10,000 reward for her safe capture, but no one has ever been able to catch her." He chuckled to himself.

Chris, the other passenger from the flight, was busy changing into running gear, but he paused to regard Smithy's story. I wasn't one for talking to strangers much, but Chris apparently was, and I had learned pretty much all there was to know about him in the short time it had taken to fly to Pendle Island. He was nice enough, but opposite to me in pretty much every way. Chris was a fitness enthusiast and described himself as 'so optimistic that my glass isn't half full, it's overflowing!'

It had been a long flight.

"Wow! That's amazing!" Chris said. "I had no idea there were wild pumas out here! This island is beautiful!"

I had to wonder if we were looking at the same island. At the moment all I could see was a cold grey lump of rock covered in mist and tarmac. And it was raining now too. Great.

"There's no way a puma could survive here," I said. "It's too cold. It's a local myth, right? To attract tourism?"

Smithy shook his head and nodded at the claw marks on the wall behind me. "Does that look like a myth to you? She's real! I've seen her! Anyway…" He looked back at the rusted pickup truck parked beside the lounge. "This is my ride. As I was saying I haven't got room to give you a lift. I've got a truck full of mannequins."

Both Chris and I looked over to see that Smithy's truck was, sure enough, full of mannequins. I had questions, but I wasn't sure I wanted to know the answer.

"There's nothing better than stretching out the old hamstrings after a long flight!" Chris crowed enthusiastically. The limber thirty-something was now squat down on the floor and twisting his legs into various pretzel shapes. We'd only been off the plane for five minutes, but Chris had somehow already changed into workout gear and he was wearing a ridiculously large backpack. He jumped up onto his feet, took a large breath of the cold morning air and pointed at a random spot in the mist. "That way."

"You're meeting someone?" Smithy asked, eyeing the fitness enthusiast as though he was an alien from another planet.

"I came here to run the Pendle peaks! I'm a hill runner, and I'm going to tame this fierce island! It's a lovely morning for a warmup." He looked at me. "Fancy joining me, Chelsea? Do you run hills?"

"Oh, sure."

His face lit up. "Really?!"

"No, sorry Chris. I only run when there's a clearance sale on ice cream. Have fun though."

"I always do. Have a super day. It was great to meet you both!"

Without another word Chris took off into the mists and quickly vanished from sight.

Smithy turned and looked at me as though the departure was completely normal. "And that leaves you, missy. Is someone meeting you here? I don't want to leave a lady alone around these parts."

I almost scoffed. No one had ever referred to me as a *lady* before.

"My cousin is supposed to be picking me up," I said. "She's always been a little tardy. I don't mind waiting. Maybe I can even bag that puma and get myself a nice reward." It was a joke, but Smithy wasn't laughing.

"If you see that puma the best thing to do is run," he said with grave sincerity. He turned his head in interest. "You've got family on the island then? I lived here my whole life and just about know everyone. I don't remember seeing you here before. Who's your kin?"

"The Sponks," I said. There were a whole host of them from what I understood. My cousin Lizzy and I kept in touch and I wrote to my aunts every now and then, but my mother had left the island when I was young. I'd never really grown up 'in' the family.

Smithy's face turned grave. "Oh, I'm sorry. But that's odd."

I laughed. I know my family had a reputation on the island, but it was the first time someone had ever apologized for it. "What's odd?"

"I don't remember seeing a 'Sponks' on the flight manifest. There was a Chris McMillan and Chelsea Moon."

"Yes. I was born Chelsea Sponks, but my mother changed our last name after we left the island."

His eyes grew wide. "Little Chelsea Sponks! Why... I remember you now. You were just a little baby when your mother left. And that would of course make your mother Lorelai Sponks."

"Lorelai Moon," I corrected. "But, yes, that's her."

"Well then, that makes me feel much better to leave you here alone in this mist. Sponks women are as tough as they come. I'd hang around, but I've got a busy day."

"Those mannequins won't dress themselves."

Smithy chuckled. "They're for my wife. She's always up to something crazy." He turned and headed for his truck, calling back as he walked. "Good to see you again Miss Sponks! Welcome back to Pendle Island!"

"It's Moon!" I shouted back. "Chelsea Moon!"

Smithy started his truck, turned it around and stopped as he drove past me. "Ah, you can try and run from the Sponks name, but that's what you are, through and through. Be seeing you around Miss Sponks!"

"It's..." Moon, is what I wanted to say, but Smithy had already put his foot to the floor and peeled off before I could finish. Now I was alone the creepy airport seemed all the creepier. Where the heck was my cousin?

I pulled my phone out to call her and realized I didn't have any service. "Great. So, I'm ticking off all the horror film clichés," I said to myself.

Creepy mist. Huge beast on the prowl. Small white girl left by herself. What next? Werewolves on the runway?

A howl broke out across the cold morning air, and I about jumped out of my skin. It was immediately followed by the roaring of a tuned-up engine however, and in the distance, I saw bright lights breaking through the mist.

"Lizzy."

It just had to be.

Seconds later a huge black SUV with pimped out wheels broke through the mist and screeched across the tarmac. 'Bark at the Moon' by Ozzy Osbourne, howled from the SUV's open window, accompanied by an out-of-key howling that could only be my cousin Lizzy.

The tank-like vehicle came to a screeching halt a few feet in front of me. Lizzy kicked open the driver door and jumped onto the tarmac, the music still blaring from the car behind her. She was goth chic from head to toe. Her leather jacket was crossed with pointless zips, and her many piercings and dark black shades made her look like a Rockstar.

She played air guitar to the song's solo and was basically on her knees when the song came to its end. When it was over, she pulled off her shades and burst out laughing.

"Now tell me that isn't the best welcome ever," she said as she came forward to hug me.

"You were out of key," I laughed as I embraced my cousin. Lizzy had always been the wildcard growing up, and it amused me greatly to see that she hadn't changed a bit.

"Nah, no way dude. Maybe your ears were just hearing it wrong. How was the flight babes? It's so good to finally meet you in person!"

Lizzy lurched forward, burying me in a bone-breaking hug. She was small, but I was taken aback by her surprising strength. The two of us had been pen pals since we were young girls and our long-distance friendship was enhanced by video calls when the internet became a thing.

Despite all the years of talking this was the first time we'd actually met face-to-face.

"It's good to see you too," I wheezed. Lizzy released me from her grasp. She grabbed my bags and threw them into the back of her large SUV, making the cases look like they weighed nothing at all. I climbed into the passenger seat, cranked the heating up and put on my seatbelt.

"The flight was fine, the airport however…"

I glanced back at the airport as it disappeared into the mist behind us.

"Yeah, it's a relic. Truth be told most people come to the island by boat now. The harbor is much more up to date. It's only a thirty-minute boat ride to the coast. Usually it's way cheaper to fly to LAX and then sail across."

I already knew as much. I'd researched travel options for a week or two before booking my tickets to Pendle, and a direct flight had already come in way more expensive every time I'd looked. As luck had it the prices for a direct plane were slashed when I finally decided to book.

Lizzy glanced over at me. "You're wearing all black. Super. That means we can head straight there. I'm not really one for tradition, but it feels appropriate given the occasion."

I turned my head at her. As far as I knew we were just going back to her place. "What are you talking about?"

She twisted her lips slightly. "Ah… there's a chance I forgot to tell you. My bad."

"Tell me what?"

"Our great aunt Griselda died. It's her funeral this morning."

"What? That's terrible!"

"Actually, it's more of a 'ding-dong the witch is dead!' scenario. She didn't have many friends here, and that includes the family. To be honest I didn't know the old coot at all."

"Oh. I don't understand then. Why go to her funeral?"

"Because before I picked you up, I was the only one planning on going, and I don't know about you, but the thought of an empty funeral makes my heart break. Even if it is for a terrible old hag."

"I knew you were a sweetie underneath all that leather."

Lizzy laughed. "Sweet has nothing to do with it, Chelsea. There's another reason for the drop-in. I need to make sure that she's dead and not coming back."

I laughed, but this time Lizzy didn't join in. "Wait, are you serious?"

The hardened expression on her face told me that she was.

I looked out at the mists surrounding the winding main road. Chris was out there somewhere, cheerily stumbling through bracken and marveling at the cold and wet.

I was starting to think I should have joined him.

2

———

"Dearly beloved, we are gathered here today... wait. That's not right."

Lizzy and I side eyed one another as the pastor fumbled through a stack of cue cards.

"Just a sec," he laughed awkwardly. "It's here somewhere."

"He's hopeless," Lizzy muttered under her breath.

"He's a pastor, you can't say that."

"Pfft, don't be fooled by the dog collar, I went to school with that idiot. We used to call him Bill "Useless' Brown. Even the teachers joined in. He only got this job because his father is high up in the church."

I watched as the useless Pastor Brown dropped his cards. His face turned bright red and he sank to his knees to gather the cards up, laughing awkwardly all the while. I buried my head in my hands. I couldn't watch.

"At least we're not the only ones here," Lizzy said. "More turned up than I expected."

At that point I had to look around the deserted graveyard, which was, of course, still empty. It appeared that Lizzy had a strange sense of humor.

We were at the graveyard outside St. Buncubus church, sitting graveside as Pastor Brown prepared to deliver Griselda's funeral (If he ever actually found his notes.) The scene looked like something out of a movie. A light rain was sprinkling down and rows of empty foldout chairs stood on the wet grass. Lizzy had taken a seat on the fifth row, which was also at the back, pulling me in to sit beside her as I went for the front.

There was no one else here, and truth be told I also felt my heartbreak a little for poor Griselda. I knew nothing about the woman other than the vague picture Lizzy had painted on the drive over here, but even if she was a nasty old hag it didn't make an empty funeral any less sad.

"Ah, here we are!" Pastor Brown announced to the mostly empty graveyard. He looked up at Lizzy and I and blushed again. "Uh... where were we? Jean was a mother to five children, and she loved her dogs. Wait."

"Flipping heck, Bill," Lizzy said as she stood up and threw her hands in the air. "I'll do the damned service!" Lizzy's large Doc Martens stomped through the wet grass as she stormed into the rain. She pretty much pushed the Pastor aside as she commandeered his pulpit. "Be useful and sit!"

Bill nodded and ran to the front row, tripping on his gowns as he did so.

"I'll make this quick, thanks to all of those that came. I know it's a long journey to this side," Lizzy said. As Bill was the only other person here, she was mostly speaking to me, but from the tone of her voice you'd think the graveyard was full of people.

"Griselda wasn't a nice person. That much I knew. I only met her a handful of times and when I did, I was keen to get out of there. I still have a scar on my elbow from the time she shot me with her air rifle." Lizzy pulled up her sleeve and held out her elbow. I could just make out a white circle on the point of her arm.

"She would curse you for looking her in the eye. She hated the postal service and she didn't get on with anyone in the family. Her reputation as a liar, a thief, and an all-round maniac is both true and understated.

"With all that said she *was* a Sponks, and as such she will be missed. She was a mean old witch, but now she's gone she's not our problem anymore." Once again, she looked around the old graveyard as though addressing an audience. "She's yours!" Lizzy laughed. "Please, *please,* make sure she behaves. For all of our sakes I will now check that she *is* dead."

I had to hold my breath as Lizzy turned around and threw open the casket door. She wasn't kidding about making sure.

"Yep! Dead as a doornail! Hoorah! Well. That concludes the service. Thanks for coming. Crawl back to your hollows. Good day."

Lizzy skipped down off the stage, snapping her fingers at the pastor as she walked past. "That's how you deliver a sermon, *Bill,*' she jibed but then stopped to trek back to him. "Do you have the notes about the burial instructions?"

"Y-Yes!" he sputtered. "You were very specific, I couldn't forget!"

"Repeat it back to me," she said sternly.

"Nails in the coffin, and a slab of six-inch Pendle Island slate three feet below the grass!"

"Very good. See to it that the instructions are carried out without fault. My family is paying good money for this!"

"Of course!"

When Lizzy arrived back at my side, she looked relieved that the service was done. "Want some breakfast? I'm starving."

"Uh… sure," I said as I stood up to follow her back to the SUV. It was one of the weirdest funerals I'd been to, but I was also darned hungry. "Is there a wake?"

Lizzy laughed. "Heavens no. That would require friends, of which Griselda was severely lacking. Still, I'm pleased the extended family showed up."

As I followed Lizzy back to the car, I couldn't help feeling confused again. Perhaps her strange sense of humor was her own personal way of mourning, even if she wasn't that close to Griselda. Looking back at the graveyard one last time I saw pastor Bill open an umbrella into his face and nearly stumble back into the open grave. Perhaps 'useless' was a little abrasive, but Bill certainly did seem clumsy.

One thing in particular did catch my eye though as the sun started to break up the early morning mists. It was still raining lightly but shafts of misty golden sunlight broke over the hilltops and shone down into the graveyard. The golden light suffused the air and gave everything a dreamlike quality.

The light, mist, and rain must have combined together to create an optical illusion, because in that moment I swore I could see hundreds of translucent figures, mostly women, leaving the graveyard and floating back through the air in all directions.

"I'm more jetlagged than I thought," I said as we got into Lizzy's car. "I just imagined a crowd of ghosts."

Lizzy shot me a quizzical look as she turned the SUV back onto the main road. "What?"

"Ghosts," I said. "Or see-through people at least. I think it was a trick of the light. It was weird."

A few seconds of silence passed before Lizzy pulled her SUV over on the side of the road. She put the vehicle in park and turned to examine me through her squinting eyes. "You're serious."

"It was probably an illusion, like I said. And I am tired from the red-eye flight. Smithy was nice, but I was trapped with this other guy that really liked to drone on."

"No, I mean. You *can't* see ghosts?"

Ah. She was being weird again. "Look Lizzy, I know you may be grieving and all, and a quirky sense of humor is a perfectly fine way of mourning—"

"I'm not grieving you bat, and I'm not joking around! What do you mean you can't see ghosts? There were hundreds at the funeral."

I blinked. "Wait. So you saw them too? That wasn't a trick of the light? I only saw them for a second. Does that mean they were real? Does that mean…"

Ghosts were real?

Lizzy was looking more confused by the second. "I did think your aura felt a little sleepy. I figured you were just abstaining from magic. Did Aunt Lorelai seriously not tell you for all these years?" She was more talking to herself at this point, which didn't clear up any of the confusion.

"Tell me what? Is my mom hiding something?"

A hearty laugh bellowed from Lizzy's throat. "Oh, you could say that. You have a *lot* to catch up on. Like a *lot*. Spending some time here on Pendle Island is certainly going to open your eyes to a lot of things."

"To ghosts?" I said, still trying to understand what was happening.

"You're a witch, Chelsea. Griselda was a witch. I'm a witch. Your mom is a witch. Every last mad bat in our family is a witch."

I stared at my cousin for a few seconds as I waited for the punchline. "Lizzy, as I said, mourning is different for everyone, so—"

Lizzy snapped her fingers and her entire appearance changed. Her goth chic style instantly transformed and bright colors whirled around her body until she looked like a fifty's housewife. Her straight dark black hair was now platinum blonde curls and she was now wearing a turquoise blue housewife dress with polka dots. A string of large white pearls glistened around her neck and her black lipstick change color until it was bright red. She looked great.

"How on earth did you—"

Before I could finish my question, she snapped her fingers again. She went from Lizzy the housewife to Lizzy the librarian. With another snap she was a hippy with dreadlocks and tie-die. Then she was a corporate businesswoman with powerful shoulder pads and a killer pants suit. With one final snap she took on her goth chic look again.

"Are you getting it yet?" she said.

"Magic is… real?" I said, sounding somewhat dumbfounded.

"Magic is real," she repeated, stating the words as fact. She put the SUV back into gear and pulled back onto the road. "I'm a witch, Griselda was a witch, and you're a witch. Every woman in our family is a witch."

I could only blink as I tried to process the information. It all felt a little unbelievable. Had Smithy crashed the plane on the flight over here? Was I dead or dreaming?

"Look I can appreciate that this is a lot to take in," Lizzy said as she looked over to see my visible shock. "The best thing to do is get some breakfast at Aztec Pancake and we can talk this over some more there."

"...Aztec Pancake?" I said, my mind still focused on the whole witch thing.

"It's the best breakfast joint of the three towns on the island. The owner is a bit whacky and everything is themed to look like Aztec ruins in a jungle."

"Sounds interesting..."

"Oh, it's the best. If anything can help you digest a bit of life-changing information, it's a stack from Aztec Pancake."

"Life-changing information?"

"The whole witch thing?" Lizzy said.

"Oh yes..." I said. I was starting to think I might actually be in shock. "I'd forgot about that."

I was confused.

I was on my way to get pancakes.

I was a... witch?

3

———————

℘izzy's SUV followed Pendle Island's coastal road and as the mists cleared up, I was treated to the island's glorious views. Maybe I'd been wrong to call it a grey lump of rock. Now the sun was out the island's natural beauty was beaming, and though I hadn't been back to the island since I was a baby, I felt as though it called up distant memories from somewhere deep within me.

We were traveling around the island in a clockwise fashion. To our left the blue sea sparkled like a blanket of sapphires. Several small beaches passed us by and at one point the road wound narrowly upwards, snaking alongside steep white cliffs which fell sharply into the sea.

To our right there was the island itself. I had spent a lot of time as a child wistfully studying the island, tracing its contours with my fingernail and wishing I could one day go back to the place where I originated from. It had always seemed so small when compared to the west coast of America, which was only a couple hundred miles away. Now that I was actually here on the island it seemed unbelievably big compared to the tiny shape I had traced with my nail all those years ago.

As great as the sights were however my mind was still running loops around the whole 'witch' thing. I kept wondering if Lizzy had a talent for quick change that I wasn't aware of, or if she had used some other trick to try and pull one over on me. I knew her well enough to know she was a practical joker.

Despite that, the outfit change and the ghosts at the funeral were too big an oddity to ignore. I still wasn't sure what to believe.

After a short drive we left the island's rural coast behind us and entered the town of Pendle itself. Before long Lizzy had parked in the lot of a diner with some very interesting design choices. She hadn't been kidding about the bold theme. The outside of the building had been kitted out to look like a crumbling Aztec ruin complete with overflowing vines. The theme continued inside as well.

We grabbed a table, ordered food and chowed down when our fresh pancakes arrived. The pancakes were stacked high, square shaped, and got progressively smaller with each ascending layer. I was eating a miniature Aztec temple made of pancakes, and I had to say they were out of this world. It was the first time I'd eaten pancakes while listening to howler monkeys in the background.

"How were the pancakes ladies?" a deep baritone voice said from behind the counter. I looked over and saw a giant man with dark skin and a pearly white smile. His apron was covered in flour and syrup stains.

"Top notch as always Neville," Lizzy said. She gestured with her hands like an Italian chef. "If I didn't know any better, I'd say you sold your soul to the devil to be the world's best pancake cook."

"The devil would have been an ideal choice. Like a chump I sold my soul to Bo Bennett."

"That's his wife," Lizzy explained to me. "She runs the joint too. Neville this is my cousin, Chelsea Sponks. She was born on the island, but this is her first time back here since she was a baby."

"The pleasure is mine Miss Sponks," he said warmly. "I trust the pancakes were to your liking?"

"I'm not exaggerating when I say I think I might be back for dinner."

Neville's loud laugh filled Aztec Pancake. Its sheer volume shook me, but it must have been a common enough sound in the diner as the regular diners didn't even flinch. "I can tell we'll get on just fine. Did that daughter of mine top up your drinks?"

"I'm doing it now, dad! Gosh!" our server said as she quickly rounded the corner with a pot of coffee. She was a young and pretty mocha-skinned girl with long chestnut hair that was pulled back in a long ponytail. She had waited on our table since arriving, and I had no complaints about her service.

"Take no notice of him, Carmel," Lizzy said as the young girl filled up our drinks. "He's just messing with you."

"Say hello to Chelsea there!" Neville shouted to his daughter from behind the counter. "She's a Sponks! She's moving to the island!"

"I uh…" I laughed awkwardly. "I'm not moving here, I'm just visiting."

Carmel flashed a pearly white smile that rivaled her fathers. "Ah, if you're a Sponks woman then the island is in your blood, through and through. It's nice to meet you." She looked at Lizzy. "You should have said she was your cousin! Why didn't you introduce me?"

"I was too busy daydreaming about your dad's pancakes. Sorry." Lizzy shrugged.

Neville returned back into the kitchen shortly after that, and Carmel was busy juggling a dozen other tables in the Aztec-themed diner, which left Lizzy and I to our coffee.

"So…" I said very slowly as I traced my finger over the lip of my cup. "The witch thing."

Lizzy snapped out of a daydream, looking like she had completely forgotten about our bombshell conversation from earlier.

"Right. Hang on a sec." She looked around quickly and then snapped her fingers. All sound ceased. The pre-recorded sounds of jungle ambience vanished. The clatter of forks, Neville's laughter, and the babble of background conversation disappeared. I could only hear my breath, and the sound of Lizzy's fork as she ate the last of her pancakes.

It was eerily silent.

"What happened?" I said in alarm.

"Bubble of silence," Lizzy said in a very manner of fact way. "We can't hear anything outside the bubble. They can't hear anything inside. It's elementary magic. Squint and you might be able to see the bubble."

I did as she said and looked around us. Sure enough I could see a very faint bubble surrounding our table. It looked like it was about an inch thick and made of very faint cloud. I simply shook my head in amazement. "Okay, I'm starting to believe the witch thing now."

Lizzy raised a brow. "My costume change and a funeral full of ghosts wasn't enough?"

"Up until this morning I thought the 'narwhal' was the most unusual thing on this planet. You've upped the ante quite a bit with witches and ghosts."

"Narwhal?"

"Yeah, you know, the whales with horns? They're like unicorns of the sea."

She balked. "Those things are real?!"

"Right?!" I'd had to google every day for a week before I believed it. "But we're talking about witches. Not narwhal."

"I'm looking that up later. I don't believe you. But, you're right. I should fill you in. Everyone in our family is a witch, including you. Magic power flows through the Sponks bloodline, and we have the ability to harness that magic and use it to our liking."

"I don't understand, why would my mom never say anything about this?"

She shrugged. "I was the same age as you when she left the island. As far as I know she left to follow a man. Now that I know she hid your magical heritage from you, I'm starting to think there's more to that story."

I already had the feeling this was a conversation that was going to bring up more questions than answers. Why would mom keep something like this from me? Although a thousand questions were already burning on my tongue, I let Lizzy carry on. I didn't want to distract her now she was actually talking.

"You may recall some moments in your life when odd things have happened that you can't explain."

"More and more recently since getting here."

She laughed. "Get used to it. Pendle is a magnet for odd. My point is that this is a natural consequence of you being magical. Our power is strong and it will find an outlet if not used often enough."

I shook my head. "I don't know, I'm starting to think maybe I'm just not magical. That's probably why mom left with me as a child."

If I was the first non-magical girl in a long family line it made sense, she would be ashamed of it.

"Yeah, I'm not buying it," Lizzy said. "Although your aura is sleepy, I can tell there's something powerful in there. You're a witch, just like me, you just have to learn."

"How do I—" I paused at seeing Carmel standing next to our table. It looked like she was shouting to get Lizzy's attention. "Uh, Lizzy?" I nodded to Carmel.

"Oh, bugger!" she said. She snapped her fingers under the table and the din of Aztec Pancake came back as a deafening wall of sound.

"What was that?" Carmel mused. "I was shouting at y'all, but I couldn't hear a word you were saying."

Lizzy groaned to herself. "Uh. Sorry to do this Carmel." She placed a hand on Carmel's and then in a loud Italian accent shouted, "Fuhgeddaboudit!"

For a few seconds I thought the bubble of silence was back. I looked around and saw everyone in the diner sitting blankly, staring ahead as though they had turned to standby mode.

"Lizzy," I whispered. "What the bloody hell is going on?"

"*Forget about it.* It's a spell to patch up mistakes. I made it myself," she said. "My spell craft is a little hokey, but this is my masterpiece. Give it a second."

Sure enough the café's din resumed and Carmel carried on as though she hadn't seen anything unusual.

"Hey Lizzy, sorry to disturb you, but there's a guy asking after you at the door. Should I tell him you're here?"

Lizzy cautiously turned around in her booth while trying to spy the man asking after her. From our position we couldn't see him.

"Is he cute?"

"He's wearing a suit?" Carmel shrugged.

"Normally I would tell you to turn a suit away, but my intuition is saying otherwise today. Send him over." Carmel went over to fetch the man, and Lizzy leaned into whisper to me. "That's one of your first lessons, always trust your witch intuition. Something tells me this is important."

Carmel came back a moment later and then returned to her tables. The young man who had followed her was quite slim, but tall, and he had a rather handsome face. He *was* cute.

"Lizzy Sponks?"

"Who's asking?" Lizzy said suspiciously.

"My name is Jack Valentine," he said and held out his hand. Lizzy fist bumped it.

"Break a lot of hearts?"

"I work in law, so yes."

"Touché. It's not often that lawmen are calling for me by name. Can't you give me a customary five second head start while I run out back?"

Jack chuckled, his sharp green eyes flourishing with warmth. "Actually, I have come to settle your aunt's estate. I was advised you might be able to help."

"Griselda mentioned me in her will?"

"Uh, well, yes and no. She had a will by exception."

"A what?"

"She specifically named all the people she did *not* want her will to go to in any circumstances." Jack pulled a scroll from his pocket and let it flap out onto the table. Lines of chicken scratch cursive scrawled across the grey-brown parchment. "Griselda was sure to name every relative, dead and living, who was *not* to receive any of her estate."

Lizzy turned to me and shook her head in disbelief. "She really was an angry old crow." She looked back at Jack. "I'm not sure I understand. Why did you need to seek me out if Griselda cut everyone in the family out of her will?"

"Well that's just the thing, a will by exception is a very specific thing. It's an archaic legal document. People don't use them often because they can be problematic. If a recipient on the list changes their name, before the deceased passes, they effectively are still within the will, if they are in relation."

"Okay..."

"The interesting thing in this case is that only one person in your family has ever changed their name legally. Do you happen to know a 'Chelsea Moon'?"

Lizzy's mouth dropped to the table and she pointed at me. "She's Chelsea Moon!"

Oh, so *now* I was a Moon and not a Sponks.

Jack's eyes widened and he stared at me in surprise. "Well! That certainly makes my job easier. What do you say Miss Moon, would you like to accompany me and discuss your inheritance?"

I stared at Jack and Lizzy in disbelief and found that words had failed me again. I was sure it wasn't the last time it would happen today.

This day was just getting weirder and weirder.

4

Perhaps it was my 'witch intuition' speaking, but something told me it was worth hearing the lawyer-type out. As I had been off the island for most of my life and was more extended family than close, I thought it would be best if Lizzy accompanied me to check out the will.

"Want to come?" I said to her.

"Ugh… I mean I'm dying to find out what you've inherited. Griselda was such a shut in that the latter part of her life was a mystery." She huffed. "I'll have to pass though. I was supposed to run some errands after picking you up from the airport. Why don't you go, and we'll catch up back at mine later? I can pick you up again if you need another ride."

With that Lizzy and I parted ways at Aztec Pancake. I climbed into Jack Valentine's shiny white Mercedes and buckled up as he took off.

"It's occurring to me just now that you could be anyone," I said to him.

"Like an axe murderer? There's more money in law. You can google me if you need assurance. Be wary though, the internet on this rock is slow."

I kind of wanted to, but it felt a little rude doing so right in front of

Jack's face. After all my intuition was telling me that he was not a threat, though it felt a little weird that I was already making decisions based off invisible feelings. I still didn't have service anyway. I couldn't look him up even if I wanted to.

"I trust you; I think. An axe murderer wouldn't drive a Mercedes. He'd be too worried about getting blood on the seats."

"You seem to know a lot about axe murderers. Maybe I should be the one that's worried?"

I laughed. For a lawyer he seemed all right.

A short and mostly silent car ride later we were on the other side of town. Jack parked up outside a fancy-looking hotel and stopped the engine.

"Uh…" I said as I stepped out of the car and looked up at the hotel. It looked like the kind of place that was way outside my budget. There was a porter in tops and tails outside the front, carrying bags for a wealthy looking elderly couple.

"Careful with that bag!" the old woman snapped at the porter. "It's antique alligator skin! They don't make them like that anymore!"

The unfortunate porter bumbled his apologies and the group made their way inside. I looked at Jack.

"You've brought me to a hotel, I thought we were heading to your office," I said.

"My office is in here. I'm actually a sit-in representative for Gild Group, the company that owns this string of luxury hotels. In my free time I dabble in estate law as well. Follow me!"

I followed Jack inside.

The lobby was a tall and open room with checkered marble flooring, trickling fountains and tall stone pillars that ran all the way up to the ceiling. Gilded portraits and expensive sculptures were dotted around the room. Up ahead I could see the elderly couple from outside. The woman, who was wearing heels, pearls and a large fur coat, was currently lambasting a girl at the reception desk.

"And I want him fired!" she shouted, her shrill voice echoing around the hall. "Do you know how hard it is to find alligator skin these days? Do you know who I am?! I am Elizabeth Montague!"

Jack's eyes widened as we walked past the desk. "This way," he said in a low voice as we entered a long corridor branching off from the lobby. Once the doors shut behind us, he let out an exasperated sigh as though he was glad to be clear of the scene.

"She seemed… delightful," I said.

"Oh, Elizabeth Montague? She's a character all right. Most people on this rock are friendly enough, but she's one that I try and avoid when I can. She'll pick a battle with anyone, and she's not a fan of me either."

"Why?"

"She's always trying to sue someone for something. She's come to my office a dozen times at least and I always have to pretend my caseload is full. When she finally cottoned on, I think I made it onto her list."

"She has a list?" I said.

He shrugged. "Probably not, but she seems like the type. I *allege* that she may or may not have a list."

"Careful, your mouth is dribbling lawyer talk."

"It may or may not have a tendency to do that," he said, smiling at me in a way that made my stomach flutter.

Jack's office was small, but smart. Once inside we sat down at a small mahogany desk and he jumped straight into things. He started by listing Griselda's personal effects.

"There was a few thousand dollars in Griselda's checking accounts when she died. She did have a house and she owned it outright. That is now yours."

I blinked in disbelief. "I own a house?"

He slid a picture across the table to me. It showed a bright blue, three-story, Victorian house. It looked beautiful. "I can't believe this!"

"Believe it," he said with a smile. "It's yours." He passed a set of keys across the table too.

"312 Cherry Road," I said as I read the address on the tag.

"Huh?" Jack looked up from the paperwork. "Ah. No. That's three and a half, Cherry Road."

"I didn't realize house numbers could have halves."

"I looked into it because I found it odd, but the official records aren't much help. It looks like there was a border discrepancy some point in the far past. All I know is that it's perfectly legal." He passed another set of keys across.

"What are these?"

"Griselda had a boat. It's currently moored at the local dock. It's paid for annually, and it looks as though the space is up for renewal this month."

"Thanks for the heads up." I had no idea what to do with the boat. Probably just get rid of it. Using one was not in my remit.

"And that's everything," he said and dusted off his hands. "We just need to sign a few documents, and everything is taken care of. This is a fairly simple one. Open and shut. If you like I can give you a ride to the house so you can take a look around. I'm actually heading in that direction to see another client."

"Uh, sure, that would be great actually. Thanks!"

Cherry Road, as it turned out, was a steep country road that led out the north side of Pendle and climbed over one of the steep hills flanking the town. Thick forests of trees surrounded the road on all sides, and long driveways branched off from the road, leading up to houses that were set back far into the trees.

"This is you," Jack said, pulling his Mercedes into a driveway that had a large black gate across it. 'Driveway' might have been a bit generous. The path up to the house from the road was a muddy track that was just wide enough for a car.

"Fancy. Have I hit big?"

"The houses up here are nice, but old. There should be a key for the gate on the ring I passed to you."

We stepped outside of the car and I fished through the many keys on the large silver ring. None of them worked with the gate. Jack even tried, but it was no luck.

"Look, I'll just walk up. There's a spot I can walk through at the side there. You don't have to worry about driving me the rest of the way."

"You're sure?"

"Yeah. A bit of walking might do me good after all those pancakes."

"If I didn't have this meeting, I'd walk you to the house at least, but I'm running late now." Jack walked back to his car and opened the driver door. "Chelsea, I was thinking."

"Huh?"

"It might be handy for me to have your number, in case there's any follow up paperwork with the estate. There probably won't be, but if there are any troubles on your end, I might be able to help."

"I thought you said this was open and shut?"

"It is, but it doesn't hurt to be diligent."

"I suppose you're right."

I mean I'd never actually inherited anything before, so if anything troubling did come up it would be handy to stay in touch. I passed Jack my number and he handed back his business card in exchange.

"I've yet to have service on this rock. A text might be better than a call."

"Sure, and if you'd like I can show you around at some point? I know the town well and I could help you settle in over coffee."

"Ah," I said, my lips twisting in a knowing smile. "So that's why you wanted my number."

Jack just smiled back and shrugged like a mischievous schoolboy. "I'm a lawyer. Trickery is in my blood. I'll delete your number if you like. I meant it when I said there might be some more things to clean up though."

"Oh, I'm sure," I said with light sarcasm. "Let me take a raincheck on the coffee thing. I'm not saying no, I'm just jetlagged and there's a lot to process this morning. I'm only supposed to be visiting for a week or two, and now I have a house here."

We said our goodbyes, Jack left, and I made my way up the muddy track to the house at the top of the drive. Once there I was both impressed and a little confused. The house was amazing, but it was also… a dump.

"This can't be right," I said to myself. I pulled out the photo of the cheery Victorian house Jack had slipped across the desk to me and held it up to the shack before me. I didn't know how old the photo was, but the house had clearly seen its fair share of winters since then.

The bright blue paint had faded away. The roof was sagging and covered in moss. The windows were dark, dirty and grim. Even the trees surrounding the house looked forlorn.

"Well that answers any questions about staying here," I muttered as I walked onto the porch and wrestled with the ring of keys again. For a few moments I'd half considered maybe settling down in Pendle and enjoying life as the owner of a beautiful three-story Victorian.

I was not interested in some grand makeover job.

My thoughts about the house didn't improve once the door was open either. Within seconds of placing the key in the lock and stepping inside I sensed that something was wrong. The air felt cold and at the foot of the stairs I saw a column of churning black smoke levitating a foot above the old floorboards.

My heart caught in my throat. Slowly the oddity came into focus and I saw the image of an old sailor with a huge black beard. His face was fixed with an expression of utter fury. Before I could do or say anything violent torrents of wind started to blast towards me.

"Out!" the phantom roared.

Without warning it rushed at me. Something hard hit me square in the chest. I fell backwards and smashed against the floor.

Then there was a blinding flash of light.

5

The blinding flash of green light burst through the small hallway. I'd like to say I stood up and fought my corner, but I expertly adopted the fetal position instead. After a few seconds of scrunching up in a tight ball I heard a familiar voice.

"Chelsea? What's going on, are you ok?"

I looked up and saw Lizzy standing in the doorway. She helped me up to my feet. The furious phantom was now gone.

"Attacked!" I shouted. "I was attacked by a pirate ghost!"

"A pirate? Did he look mad?"

"Yes!"

"Sounds like it might have been Old Mad John. He was a famous pirate on the island hundreds of years ago. Rumor is that he was hanged somewhere around here. I wonder what he's doing in the house."

Lizzy didn't seem that plussed about the pirate ghost attack. Maybe this was just everyday news for a witch. "Man," she said as she looked around the hallway. "This place could use a little bit of elbow grease. You've got quite the task on your hands."

I scoffed and brushed dust off my dress. "As far as I'm concerned this house is yours. There's no way I have time to flip this thing before I leave in a few weeks."

Lizzy rolled her eyes. "Come on. You might stay longer than that. You came here for a reason, didn't you?"

The truth was that I came here because I didn't have anywhere else to go. Life back in the real world had become a series of dead-end jobs, and after months of monumental bad luck I was left wondering what I'd done to deserve such a crummy life. It was only when Lizzy messaged me and asked if I wanted to come visit that I finally threw my hands up and gave in. To be honest it seemed like the universe had been pushing me to come here.

I'd started to wonder if I was cursed. When I did manage to get a job, the company would go bust, and hundreds of applications for *anything* went unanswered. I even got turned down for a commission-based job selling knives door to door.

"Delaying homelessness, I suppose. I don't know what's been going on lately, but it feels like the world is out to get me. I was so desperate for money that I tried to join a well-known pyramid scheme, Lizzy."

"A pyramid scheme turned you away?"

"Then I got your message saying I should come and stay at the island for a few weeks. I used my last bit of money to fly here. Normally I wouldn't be so reckless, but—"

"Something made you do it."

"Yes!" I paused. "Do you think it was a witch? Do you think someone made me do it?" All the failed interviews. All the bad luck. Had someone forced me to come here?

Lizzy squinted at me as though she was trying to look through a dirty pane of glass. "I can't feel a curse on you. But it could very well be that it was just time for you to come home. Maybe you were meant to come back."

"So an old pirate ghost could kill me?"

"Everyone has their time," she shrugged. "Ooh. What if this is like Final Destination now? You've cheated death and now you're going to die in some whacky hot tub accident."

I stared at my cousin. "Has anyone ever told you you're weird?"

"I'm a Sponks, honey. It comes with the territory."

"Well I appreciate you saving me anyway. So, thanks."

She looked confused. "I didn't save you. What are you talking about? I saw a flash of green light when I stepped on the porch. I figured your magic had self-activated to save you. That happens sometimes in fight or flight situations."

I shook my head. "No, it definitely wasn't me. No way I could have done something like that."

Lizzy took hold of my hands and turned them over as she studied them.

"Hm. Looks like you're right. Magic leaves a trace residue on the aura, and there's nothing here." She looked around. "I wonder who saved you then?"

We both looked around the dusty old hallway and the hairs stood on the back of my neck once more. Something changed in the air then. The shadows in the house looked as though they were flickering. An imperceptible breeze moved through the room and I thought I heard several voices whispering at once.

"What was that?" I said to Lizzy.

"Something is here," she said, once again looking as though she was staring into the far distance. "I can't tell if it's good or bad."

"Is it the pirate ghost again? Should we go?"

"It's definitely not him." She held up her hands. "Wait. Do you hear that?"

A very faint tinkling sound came from the room to our left. We walked through the arched entrance into a dust-laden lounge. The house was deadly quiet, and then I heard it again. The faint tinkling came again, but louder this time.

"There!" I said and made my way over to the mantlepiece above the fire. There a small collar was vibrating ever so slightly. I picked it up and the ringing stopped. Then a muffled clattering started from the other side of the house. My intuition told me to follow it.

"Come on," Lizzy said. We left the lounge, crossed back through the hall and through another arched entrance into a fifties styled kitchen.

The sound led to a cupboard under the sink. As soon as Lizzy opened the door two metallic bowls spilled out of the cupboard and rolled across the black and white kitchen tiles until they stopped a few feet away from the wall. Both the bowls stood perfectly upright on their sides. It looked completely unnatural.

"What are they doing?" I asked.

"Waiting for something," Lizzy said, her eyes searching across the kitchen. I was still staring at the bowls when she screamed and pulled me down. "Duck!"

A cupboard behind us burst open and a rolled-up mat flew through the air and right over our heads. It slapped against the wall and dropped to the floor against the skirting board. The two bowls then resumed their journey and fell flat on the small rug.

And then a whole bunch of sounds started throughout the kitchen. A cupboard door shook to my left, and the faucets in the kitchen sink started rattling behind Lizzy.

"You get the cupboard. I'll get the sink!"

A box of kibble nearly concussed me as I opened the cupboard door, and when I turned around, I saw the faucets spitting short bursts of water into the sink. The box of kibble flew out of my hand and emptied itself into one of the metal bowls.

Lizzy and I were both looking very confused and then the collar in my hand started vibrating again. This time it was moving so fast I had to let go of it. The collar zipped through the air and looped all around the kitchen until it came to a stop in the kitchen doorway, hovering about a foot above the tiles.

A loud popping sound filled my ears and then a plume of lime-green smoke smothered the floating collar. The whole room filled with smoke until we were both coughing. When it finally cleared, we saw a small black cat sitting on the floor by the bowls.

"It's a… cat," I said absently.

"It's not a cat," Lizzy said. "It's a familiar." She stared at the small black cat. "What's your name?"

"Meow," the cat said.

Lizzy rolled her eyes. "I can take the collar off if you like. Something tells me you don't want to give up a physical body so fast."

"Okay, okay!" the cat said, its bright green eyes flaring with visible panic. "I was just kidding!"

"The cat can… talk," I said.

"It's a familiar!" Lizzy repeated. "What's your name?"

"Artemis. I was Griselda's familiar. Who are you?"

"I'm Lizzy and this is Chelsea. We're relatives of Griselda's. Chelsea inherited everything here. Which means—"

A stark realization overcame Artemis's face. I had no idea cats could be so expressive.

"She inherits me!" he wailed. "No! Another generation of Sponks servitude! I thought I was finally free! No wonder I couldn't leave!"

"Slow down," Lizzy said. "Were you the one that drove away the pirate ghost?"

"Old Man John? Yeah. I zapped him with a little magic. He wonders through here from time to time."

"You were the flash of green light?" I asked.

Artemis nodded. "When not in cat form my spirit returns to the house. I can express myself as a cloud of green smoke or a flash of green light."

"Well thank you," I blurted. I couldn't quite believe I was talking to a cat. "Why did you save me though?"

"I'm sworn to protect the house and Sponks women. If I'm being honest with you it was an automatic reflex. After Griselda died, I lost my cat form. I guess you could say I've been asleep. It feels good to be back!"

"Well thank you. I appreciate it, even if you weren't in control of your actions."

"To be honest I'm a little bit surprised. I kind of thought my soul was toast after Griselda died."

"Why would you think that?" Lizzy asked, a look of puzzlement on her face.

"Well I failed to protect her," Artemis said blankly. "That's kind of my job. Failing to do that means my soul goes to the cosmic shredder."

"Griselda died of old age," Lizzy said. "It was natural causes."

Now Artemis was the one that looked confused. I was really impressed with his ability to react.

"Uh yeah… no. Griselda was murdered. Straight up."

Lizzy was almost lost for words. "What?"

"Why don't we all sit and have a drink?" Artemis suggested. "I think we have some catching up to do."

6

Artemis had us all sit down and made us a cup of tea, or I should say Lizzy and I sorted out the tea while he ordered us around from the kitchen table.

"The kettle is on the side," Artemis said. "Fill it with water."

Lizzy took the kettle over to the kitchen sink. She turned the cold-water faucet and the whole sink hissed and shook. Water sprayed all over Lizzy and she quickly turned the faucet off again.

"Oh, don't use the faucets." Artemis licked his paw and cleaned the back of his ear. "You'll get drenched."

"Thanks for the heads up," Lizzy said. As she turned around, we saw she was drenched in water. She muttered something under her breath and a gentle curtain of steam wafted from her clothes. She was dry in seconds.

"Yeah they've been on the fritz for about a month now. The dog was supposed to fix them, but he's useless. Just get some bottled water from the fridge. Get fresh milk too. Oh, and Cookies!"

"Fresh milk?" I said. "Hasn't the house been empty for two weeks?"

"I'm not getting cookies," Lizzy said and made her way over to the fridge. She opened the door and inside I saw a bottle of water and a fresh bottle of milk.

"But I need my cookies," Artemis protested.

"No cookies. I've barely got any magic left for the day."

Artemis didn't argue the point, but when Lizzy came back to the table I had to ask.

"What does that mean?"

"Ah, I guess this is your next lesson. Magic isn't some limitless fountain you can tap into whenever you want. I'd compare it to running. There's only so far you can run in a day. The same goes for magic."

"Oh, that makes sense."

"Yes, and like running, the more you practice the better you get. I've been practicing most of my life so I can do a fair bit, but I've used quite a lot today. There are ways to charge your magic, but there's only so much you can do."

"Ways like what?"

"It's different for every witch. We can go into that another time. The point is that I'm not wasting the remains of my daily magic on cookies."

"Sorry, that's my fault," I said. I felt bad that I had somehow inconvenienced Lizzy.

"Don't be sorry. It was my choice. The costume changes were fun, and the bubble of silence was a necessity. If I'm being honest, I used most of my magic while running errands."

"But you won't get me cookies from the fridge," Artemis said flatly.

"No, I won't. And boohoo. I'm sure you'll live. You've got a bowl full of actual cat food. Maybe eat that?"

"You can use magic to get cookies from the fridge?"

"Oh sure. Anything, really. It's not like there's an unlimited supply of food popping into existence. The fridges are charmed to make easy work of grocery shopping if you want. A pack of cookies from the local store will pop off the shelf, and the money will leave my account and end up in the supermarket register. It's all very kosher."

So magic did have boundaries.

Lizzy turned back to Artemis. "Spill the beans about Griselda," she said to the cat. Artemis was currently lapping milk from a bowl. He sat up, a little white moustache over his tiny mouth.

"She left a message for me in the pond at the back. Let me finish my drink and then we'll go."

The conversation turned to idle matters as we all finished our spot of tea. Artemis was mostly interested in learning about me and why my mother had left Pendle Island in the first place. He was especially amused to hear how my name change made me the sole recipient of the will.

"Oh, that is precious!" he roared. "Griselda would hate to learn she was bested. I told her she should have just done a normal will. But she so very badly wanted to take the road more spiteful."

"I don't understand though," Lizzy said. "Didn't your mother change her name? Wouldn't she inherit the estate too?"

"That…" I blinked in surprise. "Is a very good point."

The only reason I had inherited Griselda's estate is because I was the only person in the family to change my name. But my mom was a Moon too! Why hadn't she beat the will by exception as well?

"Something smells fishy to me," Lizzy said.

"Probably the basement," Artemis said. "There's this weird mold problem down there and when it rains—"

"It was a figure of speech, Artemis," Lizzy interjected.

"Perhaps I should call Jack and clear it up," I said as I checked to see if his business card was still in my pocket. "He said there might be a few things that need straightening out. This might be one of them. If he missed my mother in his search, then that means she's now involved in this too."

I groaned. Great. The last thing I wanted was to get mom involved in this. My trip to Pendle Island was basically my attempt to delay moving back in with her while I got my life sorted.

"Lorelai the man-eater!" Artemis said with a note of fear. "She's not coming here. Is she?!"

"Artemis don't be rude!" Lizzy said.

"He's okay. Man-eater is probably an understatement. I didn't think anyone here would know about that though," I said.

"I've been Griselda's cat for sixty years," Artemis said. "I heard all about your mother as she grew up. She's still a hellcat then?"

"I think she's on her fourteenth marriage now. Put it that way."

"She's not hurting anyone," Lizzy said. "Though fourteen *is* a little excessive."

It was, and it was basically the crux of my bad relationship with mom. It wasn't like she had picked crummy boyfriends growing up. She always picked decent and respectable men as her 'partner for life' but she cycled through marriages like pairs of socks.

I was pretty certain at this point that I was a contender for a world record. Girl with most stepfathers.

Lizzy sighed. "And I can't find one good man. I'll have to call your mom and ask for tips."

"She could recommend you a good divorce lawyer or two. But actual relationship advice is probably best sought elsewhere."

"Milk is done!" Artemis shouted; his bowl now empty. "Follow me to the pond!"

Without waiting Artemis jumped off the table. Lizzy and I stared at one another as we contemplated our half-full cups of tea. The cat certainly seemed to think that everything revolved around him.

Outside we stepped back into a fine drizzle, which must have started up while we were inside the house. Artemis made me grab an umbrella off the back porch and we walked across the garden to the pond.

"See the bird bath there?" he said. "Twist the bird on top."

Lizzy did so and the pondwater started to bubble. Light and smoke appeared on the surface and a TV-sized image of an old cantankerous woman appeared in the water. She looked like a stereotypical image of an old witch. It had to be Griselda.

"Listen here cat. You better start catching more mice around here or I'm going to seriously reconsider your role as this house familiar! Don't make me bring that pirate ghost up here, and don't you think you should be exercising a bit more? You're getting a tire around the wai—"

"Twist it again!" Artemis shouted. "Wrong message."

Lizzy twisted the bird again and another message started. Griselda looked much worse this time. Dark circles sagged under her eyes and she kept looking all around as though someone was coming to get her at any minute.

"Listen to me Artemis," she whispered, fear evident in her voice. "If you're listening to this message then I'm dead or going to be dead very shortly. Someone is trying to kill me, and I think I might have an idea who is behind it. I guess you'll finally be free. I know you hate my guts, but when you're free I need you to warn the other witches that a murderer is amongst us. I—" She paused and looked somewhere out of frame. "I have to go!"

The message ended and the pondwater went back to normal. We all stood there in silence as we reflected on the message.

"When did she leave this?" Lizzy asked.

"The night before she died," Artemis said. "When I found it, Griselda was out of the house and I couldn't contact her. Shortly after that I lost my cat form and my spirit returned to the house. I knew she must have died."

Suddenly a deep voice spoke behind us. "Something in the pond?"

"Agh!" we all screamed, jumping and turning around in the air to see a giant man with an axe and a bushy beard.

"Agh!" he screamed back, seemingly just as startled by our reaction.

"Who are you?!" Lizzy shouted. She had her hands up in front of her. If I didn't know any better, she was about to use magic to attack this man.

The huge mountain man gently set his axe down and held his hands up. "Relax! I'm Adam. The groundskeeper. Griselda hired me to look after the property!"

Lizzy looked at Artemis. "Is that true?"

"Oh yeah. I see this dummy walking around here all the time," Artemis said.

"I *knew* you could talk!" Adam said as he squinted at the cat.

Lizzy regarded Adam with suspicion. "You seem pretty calm for a man that's never seen a cat talk before."

Adam scoffed. "I've seen a lot weirder. Besides, I'm not exactly the most normal bloke. I've got my own secrets. Griselda let me take the job here providing that neither one of us asks questions. I saw her practice magic from time to time."

Lizzy looked like she was about to faint with panic. "She let a non-magical know she was a witch?" She looked at Artemis. "You let this happen?!"

The cat actually shrugged. "I already told you he's a big dummy. He's not going to blab. You should see *his* secret. He—"

"I was using this axe for firewood," Adam interrupted, "but I'm not adverse to chasing you around with it."

"He's crazy!" Artemis shouted as he bolted up onto my shoulder. "Protect me!"

"Why are you still working here now that Griselda is dead?" I asked.

"My pay is in advance every quarter, and I still have a month left on this quarter. Miss Griselda has already paid for my service, so it's only fair I provide what was agreed."

"Very noble of you," Lizzy said.

"Or dumb," Artemis offered from the safety of my shoulder.

I looked over at the old sagging house. "It doesn't really look like anyone has been looking after this place."

"You're preaching to the choir. The house definitely needs work, but Griselda wouldn't let me touch it. She wanted me to take care of the grounds mostly."

There was a long garden at the back of the house. The grass was recently trimmed and *did* look like someone had been taking care of it. Beyond the pond there was a maintained vegetable garden, a fountain, and borders of tall and colorful plants.

"What's in the shack?" Lizzy asked, referring to a small structure right at the other end of the garden.

"That's his hovel," Artemis said. "The Neanderthal keeps himself chained up there. Griselda lets him live on the property."

"It's sad she died," he said, taking no notice of Artemis this time.

"She was a nice old lady. It's a shame she didn't get more visitors up here."

"You and I must have different definitions of nice," Lizzy said. "But we're grateful for you coming here. Griselda was our great aunt. Chelsea here just inherited the house."

Adam's brows lifted as he looked at me. "Oh! Then that means you're my new boss. I've just been mowing the grass on the back lawn, but if there's anything in particular you want fixing while I'm still here—"

"Please, it's okay. I've barely been here half an hour. I'm not comfortable ordering around staff. Just carry on doing whatever you like." I looked over at Lizzy and then back at the house. "I think we've seen enough here to talk some things over."

"I guess you'll be staying here now you're the owner!" Artemis said cheerfully.

"Uh…" I looked the house over again. Adam looked like a big strong guy, but I wasn't sure even he had enough elbow grease to turn this tip around. "I might have to take a raincheck on that Artemis."

"But we were just getting to know one another!" he huffed as he jumped off my shoulder. "You can't leave me here with this oaf! I'm trapped inside the property boundaries!"

"What are you going to do when your contract runs out?" Lizzy asked Adam.

"Oh, I don't know," he said, not sounding too fussed about imminent homelessness. "I'll figure something out." He looked at Artemis. "Don't worry about the stupid cat. I'll look after it."

"You will not come near me!"

"We'll be back soon," I said to Artemis, and I bent low to scratch his head. "Be nice to the big scary axe man."

"I'm going to rub my butt on his things while he's out," Artemis muttered.

"I heard that," Adam shouted.

Lizzy and I made our way back down the muddy track to her car which was parked outside the front gate. I'd have to try and find that key. My first day back on the island had quickly passed me by, and I was already feeling tired.

"I'm beat," Lizzy said as she pulled back on to the road and drove back in the direction of Pendle. "I'm thinking beers, pizza and a movie at my loft. I'll order from Pizza Palace. The pizza there is to die for. Sound good?"

"Very good," I said and melted into my passenger seat.

I had nearly finished my first day of being a witch, and I'd learned another lesson.

This witch stuff was hard.

$\mathcal{L}$izzy's place was a hip loft in the 'cool' part of Pendle. After we got back to hers, we unloaded my things from her car, ordered some pizza and chowed down while we watched old Bruce Lee movies.

When morning came, I had a much-needed shower, got changed and was greeted by the aroma of freshly made coffee. Lizzy was reading at the breakfast bar in the kitchen part of the loft.

"Morning!" I said cheerily as I entered the room.

"Morning," she grumbled back. "Don't tell me you're a morning person."

"I feel well rested. Don't you?" I shrugged.

"I'm one of those people you'd find in a 'Don't talk to me 'til I've had my coffee' t-shirts."

"You are drinking coffee…" I said. She had a plain white cup in one hand. The other was turning the pages of a giant dusty book.

"My 'coffee' is Madame Crème's fresh-baked strawberry pastries. By the way, that's our first stop on the town tour this morning. Anyway, do you want some actual coffee?"

I nodded my head and with the flick of a wrist Lizzy lazily gestured to the coffee machine on the marble countertop behind her.

The machine spat coffee into a cup and the cup floated across the air until it was on the bar in front of me.

As I took a seat at the bar, I got a better look at the book Lizzy was reading. It was about the size of a jumbo cereal box, had a thick leather cover, and its yellowed pages were glimmering with colorful runes.

"Bit of light reading?"

"I couldn't sleep last night so I started looking through some old witching books. I'm trying to figure out how we catch you up to speed with a few decades of magic. There's probably a formal process. Witch's Digest isn't much help."

"Witch's Digest?" I said.

Lizzy closed the tome and turned it around so I could read the front cover. On it there were more runes, followed by roman numerals that read 'MMLII'.

"Issue 2052," she explained. "This is an old copy. They send it digitally these days. My intuition led me to this number, but I can't find anything. We'll probably just have to speak with Mary Malkin, she's the head-witch on the island."

"You can read this stuff?" I said as I stared at the indecipherable runes.

"All witches can. You'll pick it up, don't worry." Lizzy let out a long yawn.

"What kept you up?"

"All this stuff with Griselda. I was thinking about the message she left for Artemis. Do you think it's possible someone really killed her?"

I wasn't sure.

"That's what she believed, and she asked Artemis to get the word out to other witches on the island. I feel we owe her that much at least. Is it best if we bring this to this Mary Malkin?" If she was the one in charge it seemed like the sensible thing to do.

Lizzy groaned again. "Ugh. Probably. Do we get the police involved too? I have no idea what we do in this situation."

"If she was murdered then the autopsy would have revealed something, right?"

"There wasn't one. She was old and everyone assumed it was old age. If we have to dig her up to authorize an autopsy…" She shivered.

"What?"

"Nothing. A witch's spirit can be quite powerful, and Griselda wasn't exactly a rose petal. She won't be pleased about being disturbed so soon."

"Did she have any enemies? Anyone that might have wanted her dead?" Lizzy snapped her fingers and another book flew through the air from a distant corner of the apartment. It landed on the table. It was a phonebook. "What's this?" I said.

"The phonebook for Pendle Island. It's also a list of every person on this rock that might have had a problem with Griselda."

"Oh."

"Yeah. She collected enemies; it was a hobby of hers."

On the wall behind Lizzy a moving cat clock announced loudly, "Meow! It's nine in the morning!"

Lizzy immediately perked up. "Nine! Come on! Madame Crème's is open!"

Half an hour later we were sitting at the tables outside Madame Crème's, having just finished another round of coffee with accompanying freshly baked goods. They were pretty darn terrific. With the pastries and the pancakes from yesterday, I was starting to think I might never leave this island. Lizzy now looked much more alert.

"Ah. That's better. Now, where were we?" she said with a fresh smile.

"Griselda might have had a lot of enemies," I said, "but we can probably make a list of people that had the biggest grudges against her. Wouldn't that narrow things down?"

"Morning Lizzy!" A portly man waved as he walked past.

"Morning John!" Lizzy said. As he walked by Lizzy leaned in. "See that man? Lovely chap, right? That's John Vance. He runs the biggest car dealership on Pendle Island. He sold me my Daisy."

"You called your giant SUV, Daisy?"

"The point is that he's a nice guy, and he's well-liked and trusted here."

"So?"

"So, Griselda bought a car off his dad back in the eighties before John took over the family business. The car worked fine for years. When it was about twenty years old it finally kicked the bucket and needed a lot of repair work. Griselda marched down to the dealership and was screaming at John for selling her a lemon. She took him to court!"

"She must have lost."

"She did, and that only made her more furious! I'm surprised John still acknowledges me knowing that I was related to her."

"So, Griselda had a habit of making trouble of herself."

"Now maybe you'll understand why it's next to impossible to narrow down a list of suspects."

I watched the main street of Pendle grow busier as people started their day and I felt a little deflated with the task ahead of us. Griselda certainly wasn't making this easy.

"Now this little island might not look like much," Lizzy said, "but there are a few cool things I can show you. If we get some of these tasks out the way, we can get to the fun stuff."

"I agree." I was excited for Lizzy to show me around the island, but it felt like our obligation to Griselda was more pressing at this point. "Maybe we should talk with the police first? Could I borrow your phone on the way? There's a call I need to make. I'm still not getting any service."

"You'll have to get a GoCrow SIM," Lizzy said. "It's the only carrier that works on this rock. We can add that to our list of things to do. Who are you calling?"

"Jack. I need to tell him that my mother changed her name too. If he missed that then there might be other issues with the inheritance. If I'm lucky maybe I don't have to deal with the house after all."

While Lizzy drove across town to the police station, I tried Jack several times, but the line rang out each time.

"Busy saving the world," said his answering machine. *"Leave a message."*

"Jack it's me, Chelsea. The girl from yesterday? The one that inherited the house on Cherry Road? We were joking about axe murderers?" I was rambling. Why was I rambling? "Anyway, I think there might be an issue with the will. Call me back and I can explain. Thanks."

I handed Lizzy her phone back and noticed she was smirking at me from the driver seat.

"What?"

"You like the suit," she laughed.

"I do not!"

"You were totally nervous! You like him!"

I felt my cheeks flushing red. "Well he is cute. I think he asked me out yesterday too."

"Well that settles it. You have got to go out with him. A little fling on your vacation is exactly what you need."

"I don't know. I don't want to become my mother."

Watching my mother flit from man to man over the years had really made me wary of settling down with anyone at any point, *ever.* She wasn't a black widow or anything malicious like that, but she was a sucker for love, and she got hurt over and over. It was enough to put me off dating altogether, and as such I'd never really had an actual boyfriend.

"You are single, right?" Lizzy asked.

"Perpetually. It's safer that way."

She side-eyed me. "You're not one of these 'never-been-kissed' types, are you?"

"Aren't we supposed to be solving a murder?"

"Pfft," Lizzy blew air through her lips. "We'll report it. I'm not solving it. We've got other stuff to do." With that she pulled her truck into a parking spot and we got out.

We were now by the town square. A large square park across the road from us had long terraces of fancy-looking buildings bordering it on all sides, though they were set quite far back from the road itself.

Lizzy led us into the police station and up to the reception, where a woman with curly black hair and large bottlecap glasses greeted us with little enthusiasm.

"Yes?"

"We need to speak with someone," Lizzy said. "We have a suspected murder."

The woman actually lifted her head to look at us this time and she sighed upon seeing Lizzy. "Lizzy Sponks. Elaborate?"

"My great aunt Griselda was murdered!" Lizzy slapped the desk. "Let's move Brenda!"

"Take a seat in the waiting area and someone will be with you shortly." Brenda glowered at Lizzy.

The waiting room was empty, but despite that we were still in there for nearly twenty minutes before an officer came out. He was tall, as wide as a fridge and had blazing red hair. After a quick word with the receptionist and he turned our way. He walked over.

He was strikingly handsome, with deep green eyes, a strong jaw and a thick red moustache. Normally I wasn't too bothered about moustaches, but *yowzah.*

"Lizzy Sponks," he said as though the name had crossed his lips many times. "You're not someone I want to see first thing in the morning."

"Good to see you too, Deacon," she said sarcastically.

The tall handsome man looked at me. "I don't believe we've met," he said and took my hand. As he did sparks burst across my skin. "My name is Deacon Long. I'm the Sheriff here on Pendle Island."

"Chelsea Moon, I'm Lizzy's cousin. I'm just visiting the island."

"Listen Deek we've got a problem. It's about Griselda. We think she was murdered."

Deacon stared at Lizzy, though he didn't seem that surprised by her outburst. Lizzy had mentioned that Sponks women were notorious on the island. Was this just another day for the sheriff?"

"My office," he sighed. "Now."

Deacon's office was a medium size room, with a large corner desk and an ancient computer. We all took a seat and he pulled out a notepad and pen.

"Resume," he said while taking a sip of his coffee.

"Aren't you going to offer us a drink?" Lizzy asked.

"I don't want you here for that long. Now what have you got to say?"

Charming.

"Griselda left a message at her house saying her life was in danger," Lizzy said. "You need to see it, Deacon. She looks terrified and she was scared for her life."

I paused. How on earth were we going to show a magical pond message to Deacon?

"Did she say anything about this to you before she died?"

"She didn't talk to anyone in the family. You know what she was like!"

His hand moved across the page as he took notes. "Okay. Anything else that might make you think she was murdered? What happened with her estate?"

"Um," I cleared my throat. "I inherited everything. She had an odd will and a legal loophole meant my name change left me as the sole heir."

"Name change. You're married?" he said and looked up at me.

"No, my mother is crazy."

He nodded and wrote something else down. I wanted to see that notepad badly.

"So?" Lizzy said, clearly anxious for something to happen. "Are you going to do something?!"

"Well I'll need to see the message first. Do you have it on you?"

"No, it's back at the house."

"Then I'll have to come see it. What is it? A note?"

"A… *video*," Lizzy said carefully.

Deacon looked up. "You don't sound sure."

Lizzy hesitated and looked at me.

"We might have lost it," I said quickly.

Deacon squinted at me. "You *lost* a video?"

"We have it," Lizzy said quickly. "But it's a long drive just to see a message. We can bring it here."

He regarded us both now with some suspicion. "What's going on here?" he said. "Is there something up at that house you don't want me to see?"

"Look, we just want to know that there isn't a killer on the loose," I said. "There wasn't an autopsy when Griselda died, because everyone assumed that she died of old age. Could we perhaps dig up the body and have a coroner look at it?"

"That would be an exhumation," Deacon said, "and we'd need a judge to sign off on it. You need a damned good reason to do one."

"Could this message be a reason?"

"Possibly, providing you haven't lost it."

"We have it!" I said. From the corner of my eye I watched Lizzy carefully as she moved her hands under the table. I really didn't want her to use the *'Fuhgeddaboudit!'* spell on Deacon, but I couldn't say why. Blanking the memory of everyone in a diner seemed like one thing, messing with the police seemed like another thing all together.

"You have a video message, which is your only piece of evidence that your relative might have been murdered, and you didn't bring it?"

"Well the problem is that it's in a pond," Lizzy said.

That did it. Deacon's expression changed from polite interest to annoyance. I couldn't blame him. We should have put more thought into this before turning up at his office without evidence.

"Look Lizzy, I've got better things to do then run around chasing pranks. Wasting police time is an offence, you know? You have ten seconds to leave my office before I write you up." He shook his head as we both scrambled to our feet. "I thought you'd left these childish antics behind, and you!" His blazing green eyes narrowed on me. Eep. "You're new here, so I'll give you a pass, but if I find you running around causing any more trouble, we're going to have problems. That clear?"

"Yes! Sorry! I like your moustache. Bye!"

We both ran out of the police station like naughty children who had just been chastised by the principal. A minute later Lizzy was behind the wheel and we were back on the road again.

"You like his moustache?"

"I don't know if you realized Lizzy, but that didn't exactly go well. Without Deacon we have no hoping of getting an exhumation. My compliment was a thimble of water on a bridge that is quickly burning."

"Fair enough. I should have known better than going to Deacon without everything prepared. He's a real crank when he wants to be."

"What did he mean when he mentioned childish antics? Have you both got a history?"

"Romantically? Ew, no. Deacon likes to think he sees the best in people, and I think my current lifestyle choices disappoint him greatly. He thinks I fall far of my potential. Unfortunately for him I like causing mischief and getting into trouble, so what's a girl to do?"

That meant Deacon was more of a father figure or older brother to Lizzy then, even if they were somewhat estranged. For some reason I was glad to learn there wasn't a romantic connection, but I didn't really know why. I didn't like Deacon.

Did I?

"Don't worry, Chelsea," Lizzy grinned at me from the driver's seat. "I'm not going to take your mustachioed knight in shining armor away from you!"

"What does that mean?"

"Oh, come on. You've totally found another crush and we're barely on day two. Maybe your mother's tiger blood swims through your veins after all?"

"I don't like him. I was just trying to ease his temper."

"Liar, liar, pants on fire!" Lizzy taunted.

I rolled my eyes at Lizzy's childishness. If she kept going there *would* be a murder to report today.

8

Next on our list was a visit to Mary Malkin.

Lizzy took a road leading outside of the western side of town and kept driving until turning onto a long gravel track. The track wound upwards through a forest of silver birch trees and opened onto a farm that immediately made me think of a cult. A large farmhouse was at the center of the property, and on the right between the yard and the open fields eleven freight containers had been assembled as a makeshift village of sorts.

As we pulled up the front door opened and a small woman with long silver hair walked backwards towards us. We met halfway between the truck and the front door and she turned around. I gasped.

Mary Malkin had long silver hair that was parted down the middle, grey eyes and the *only* item of clothing she was wearing was a long-faded t-shirt from the nineties with a photo of David Hasselhoff, and the words 'Don't Hassle the Hoff' printed upon it. The oversized shirt came down to her knees. Thankfully.

"Saw you coming," she said. "What's happened?"

"It's Griselda," Lizzy answered. "We found a message in her pond saying she was murdered."

Mary looked up at the sky for a second and nodded. I turned to see what she was studying, but I only saw clouds.

"Yah," she said after her moment of reflection. "Sounds about right. What do you want me to do about it?"

I looked down at her feet, which were caked with mud up to her ankles. "We want to exhume the grave so we can do an autopsy to establish cause of—"

"Chelsea Sponks," she said. "Twenty-nine years, three months and eleven days since you were last on this island." She crouched low and placed her hand into the dirt. "The island is glad you're back. But where's your mother?"

"She just met a guy."

Mary smirked and stood up again. "That she did." Her silver eyes turned on me. They felt cold and dissecting, as though they saw everything there was to see. "You want to know how to get the police onboard."

"It's Deacon Long," Lizzy said. "He's non-magical. We can't show him a talking pond."

"Aesop."

"Aesop?" I said.

"Aesop's Video Store?" Lizzy asked.

Mary nodded. "He'll help. What else did you come here for?"

"I uh…"

"Lorelai never told Chelsea she was a witch!" Lizzy said. "She needs to catch up and I have no idea what to do."

"Ah, yup. She left you in the dark on that one, huh?"

"Uh… yes?"

Mary Malkin once again squinted at the air beside us. I caught Lizzy's eyes while we waited for the head witch to finish… *whatever* it was she was doing. Lizzy shrugged back at me as if to say she had no idea either.

"You need to figure this…" She waved her hand about. "*Thing* out first. Once you're done with that we can proceed with some training. If I'm being honest it's all already in there anyway." She held her hand out and placed it against my chest.

"But what about books? Spells? Lessons? How do I learn it all?"

"That stuff is all junk. But it can be helpful. Focus on following your intuition for now. That's the most important thing you can do. Was there anything else?"

Lizzy shook her head to say no, but I did have one more question. "Yeah. Why were you walking backwards?"

Mary smiled. "I accidentally cursed myself with a temporary walk-back charm. I'm stuck like this for the next twenty-four hours." She looked into the air again. "I've got to go. A bird is about to hit my front window."

Sure enough a small kestrel bolted into the glass of the second story window and dropped onto the dirt yard. Mary walked backwards towards the stunned animal and scooped it up.

"Aesop!" she shouted at us. "Intuition!"

She walked backwards up her stairs and shut the front door behind her, leaving Lizzy and I to regard one another in confused silence.

"That was weird and intense," I said. "Is she always like that?"

"That was actually pretty normal for Mary," Lizzy said. "Just consider yourself lucky she didn't have her chainsaw."

Aesop's Video looked like it had stepped right out of the eighties. Its tall red-neon sign was deliciously retro, and inside I was delighted to find ugly patterned carpets, shelves of films to browse, cool movie posters, and film memorabilia all across the room.

"This place is... awesome!" I said through a huge smile. "I can't even remember the last time I stepped into a video store. How did this shop survive the internet?"

"Well it helps that we don't have internet on Pendle Island."

I froze. "What?"

That might have been the most terrifying thing I'd heard since arriving here.

Lizzy burst out laughing. "I'm kidding. We have it, but we're basically still on dial up here. We're supposed to get high-speed internet at some point, but the mayor has been banging that drum for over ten years. Pendle is connected, but it's so slow we can't stream video or films. It sucks, but I guess we read more books than the average town."

"So that's how a video store survives the twenty-first century."

"Yeah, and they get VHS and DVD copies from the major streaming platforms. I'm so hipster I watch all my Netflix on VHS."

"I'm not sure if I love or hate this town," I mused.

"Welcome to the club."

We walked over to the desk where an old man was sat on a high stool behind the counter. He had a large flat cap and his face was a sea of deep wrinkles. He grimaced upon seeing Lizzy.

"I already told you we don't have Jet Ski Zombies 4! I'll call when the delivery comes in!"

"Relax," Lizzy said with a dismissive hand. "This is my cousin, Chelsea. She's visiting. Chelsea this is Aesop, the old coot that runs this place."

"I suppose you're a pain in the ass too!" he shouted in my direction.

"I like your store?" I said, not sure what else to say.

Aesop smiled. "I'm just yanking your chain girlie. Pleasure to meet you." He looked back at Lizzy. "So, what can I do for you?"

"I'm showing Chelsea around town and I was busy telling her about Skeeter. Is he around?"

"Course he is! The fat pig is probably sleeping again." Aesop turned around and shouted through an open door behind him. "Skeeter! Get your fat behind out here!"

"Who is Skeeter?" I whispered to Lizzy.

She smiled. "You'll see."

A few moments later the fattest racoon I have ever seen in my life waddled through the door. It had barely taken ten steps before falling into a sitting position. A morbidly obese raccoon was the last thing I was expecting to see today—besides an actual living, breathing video shop—but the most surprising thing was his attire.

"Just to clarify I'm not going mad," I said, "we can all see a fat racoon in a sailor outfit, right?"

Aesop bent down and groaned as he lifted the enormous raccoon onto the glass countertop. It lifted its tiny little hand and snapped its fingers. A sharp wind burst through the VCR shop and I looked around to see that everything, including Aesop, was frozen.

"What does the placard on the wall say, Lizzy?" the fat raccoon said to my cousin.

"What?" Lizzy said.

Skeeter stood and pointed at the sign on the wall behind Aesop. It was a 'rules' board for the shop: 'Be kind, rewind.' 'Return on time.' 'Always pay your late fees.'

"What. Does. The. Sign. Say?" Skeeter repeated. Lizzy mumbled back the sign to him. "So, we can rule out bad eyesight then!" the raccoon shouted. "Because I was starting to wonder why you have such a hard time following the rules."

"I'll—" Lizzy started, but Skeeter interrupted, he clearly had some stuff he wanted to say.

"Fifteen overdue titles! Eighty dollars in late fees! Never rewound a single tape! Do you think I'm running a charity here?"

"Okay, okay! I'll bring your films around tomorrow along with the late fees. Just chill! I thought you were cool man!"

"I'm a wizard trapped in the body of a morbidly obese racoon," he said flatly. "And I have to stay on top of the bottom line in this store because Aesop sure as hell won't."

Skeeter pulled a small tub of butter popcorn from the thin air and started chomping down.

"You weren't morbidly obese when you first got that body," Lizzy muttered.

"I'm a racoon with access to unlimited popcorn. You try and maintain a beach body in this environment!" He purred to himself while chewing the buttery kernels. "Now, what can I do for you?"

"Mary sent us. We need help converting a pondwater message to a medium that a non-magical can see. Can you do that?"

"Sounds easy enough." The fat racoon shot a look at me. "Why are you staring?"

"Sorry, I'm just new to this whole talking animal thing. I was raised non-magical."

He nodded to himself. "Don't feel too bad. I know I'm a spectacle. What's so important about this message?"

Lizzy and I caught the fat raccoon up with everything that had happened so far. As we told the story his beady little eyes glazed over and he shoved popcorn into his mouth while he played audience.

"Ooh! Mystery afoot! How exciting. This old town could do with a bit of spice."

"She was our aunt, Skeeter," Lizzy said.

He shrugged. "And I'm a jerk wad racoon. What are you going to do about it?"

"Can you help us?" I asked. "It would mean a lot to us if you could. Please?"

"Take a lesson, Lizzy," Skeeter said as he pointed a tiny finger at me. "Your cousin has manners. I guess the apple does fall far from the tree. Ha!"

Lizzy pushed her finger into the bridge of her nose. "Can you help or not?"

"I can, but you're going to return all the tapes you owe and you're going to pay your late fines too. And you're going to rewind every tape on unwound mountain." He jerked a thumb to a wall of several hundred VHS tapes.

Lizzy groaned. "Fine! When can you come and convert the message?"

"Come by again later tonight when the shop's closed. Aesop always falls asleep by ten. I can sneak out then."

With our plan set in motion we left the shop and decided to head over to Aztec Pancake to get lunch. On the drive there, Lizzy's phone rang. "Ew!" she said, quickly throwing the phone across the car to me. "It's your suit. He's calling!"

"Hello?" I said.

"Chelsea? It's Jack. I just got your message. Sorry I missed you, I was in court. What's up?"

"I think there might be a problem with the legal loophole in the will. It might be easier to explain in person. Could I come by your office and clear some things up?"

"I'm actually out for the rest of the day, I'm helping the council with a few legal things."

"You work for the hotel, dabble in estate law and help out with the council?"

"What can I say, there aren't a lot of lawyers on this rock. I like to help when I can. I'm stuck in meetings all day until this evening. Would you like to get dinner later? My treat."

"I—" I was about to agree when I remembered we had just made plans. "I can't tonight, I'm sorry. I've got… a thing to do."

"Uh oh, not a thing."

"I'm not jerking you around, I promise. I have got another arrangement, but I can't really say what it is."

What was I supposed to say? *I can't come out tonight, I'm jailbreaking a fat sailor racoon out of a VHS shop so he can convert a pondwater message to DVD.*

"Relax, I appreciate the offer is a little last minute. You've just arrived on the island. You probably have tons of family to catch up with. I'm back in the office tomorrow, but the offer for dinner is still available if you'd rather talk somewhere more relaxed."

I bit my lip as he extended another offer my way.

"Dinner sounds good," I said after a long and hesitant breath. "What were you thinking?"

9

Later on, after the sun had set over Pendle Island, Lizzy and I made our way back to Aesop's video store to pick up Skeeter for our top-secret mission. He had given us specific instructions to meet him around the back of the store at ten.

"Where is that fat little rat?" Lizzy said as she looked through the SUV's front window. The alleyway behind Aesop's was as picturesque as you might expect. There were large dumpsters, a rusted metal door which was locked shut, and large air conditioning units.

"Wait! There! What was that?" I said, pointing to an airduct above the metal door. It popped out of the wall and dropped to the floor. A fat shape squeezed out of the small duct, fell through the air and slapped onto the concrete steps behind the shop. It stood up.

It was Skeeter.

I opened my door and helped Skeeter up and into the SUV. The fat racoon scurried over me with little grace, moved into the back and buckled himself into the booster seat that he had requested.

"You took your time," Lizzy said as she pulled off. "What was the delay?"

It was nearly half past ten now, we'd been waiting on Skeeter for thirty minutes.

"I forgot there was a game on. Aesop always stays up a little later on game night. Also, I had to change."

I looked back at the little racoon strapped into the booster seat. He wasn't wearing his sailor outfit anymore. He now had a little tracksuit on, and he was carrying a small backpack that looked like it might fit a teddy. Cute might be the word, but I wasn't sure how Skeeter would react to that description, so I kept it to myself.

In another twenty minutes we had arrived back at Griselda's house. "Wait here," I shouted to Lizzy as we pulled up to the locked gate at the bottom of the mud track. "I'll see if Artemis or Adam know where the key for this gate is."

As I walked up the muddy track in the dark, I felt a pang of fear as the house came into view. What if the old mad pirate ghost was going to attack me again?

My fears dissipated a little when I saw lights on in the house. Now that I knew Artemis and Adam were here, I felt a little bit more at ease about entering the haunted looking shack.

The front door was unlocked, and as I entered the house, I found Artemis and Adam in the kitchen, sitting at the table and playing a boardgame.

"Seven spaces!" Artemis shouted. "I rolled a seven! Move me seven spaces!"

"I moved you seven spaces!" Adam shouted back. "You were in the haunted crypt. Now you're in the cursed swamps!"

"How dare you take advantage of my disability!" Artemis roared back. "You think you can take advantage because my little paws can't move the pieces! Shame on you, dog! Shame!"

"Uh, hi guys," I said delicately from the kitchen door. "Having fun?"

Both Artemis and Adam looked up, seemingly surprised to see me.

"You're back!" Artemis said through a broad smile. "I thought I was trapped here with this oaf forever!" The cat skipped down from his spot at the table and sauntered over to nuzzle my leg. I wasn't really a cat person, but I appreciated Artemis' friendly welcome.

"Hey, what about the game?" Adam said.

"Bah, I was cheating anyway. I've got like five ghoul tokens under the cushion on my chair."

Adam deflated and started packing the game away. "That's the last time I try and entertain you, cat."

"He's a sore loser," Artemis whispered. "Have you come to stay the night? It'll be so much fun! We can have a sleepover and drink hot cocoa."

"We've come to get the message out of the pond. We need to show it to the police so we can start looking into Griselda's death. Is there a key for the gate at the bottom of the drive?"

"Key…" Artemis said to himself slowly. He looked back at Adam. "Sounds like something the Neanderthal would know about."

Adam stared daggers back at Artemis then looked at me with a kinder expression. "I've got the key for the gate. I'll go down and open it for you now."

Five minutes later Lizzy and Skeeter joined us in the kitchen.

"Is that racoon wearing a tracksuit?" Adam said as Lizzy and Skeeter stepped in.

Skeeter simply took one look at Adam and hissed.

"Skeeter!" Lizzy shouted.

"Sorry. I don't like the smell of him at all."

"Great," Adam sighed. "Another talking animal with an attitude problem."

Skeeter's shiny little eyes moved to Artemis. "Artemis," he said with a nod.

"Skeeter," Artemis nodded back.

Lizzy turned her head. "You two know each other?"

"All the familiars on the rock gather once a week in Astral Alley for our familiar book club," Artemis explained. "This week we're reading Dreadlock Astronaut."

"I thought you were contained to the boundaries of the house?" I said to Artemis.

"Oh, I am. Astral Alley isn't a physical place. I can go anywhere I like on the Astral realm though. Why do you think I sleep so much?"

"Because you're a lazy cat," Adam said.

He twisted his tiny cat mouth in a disapproving manner. "While true, it's also because I'm venturing in the Astral."

"I feel like there's so much I don't know," I said with a deflated sigh.

"I'm sure you'll catch up in no time," Artemis said, but he didn't sound so sure.

"The astral realm is a layer of existence close to ours," Lizzy said. "Witches and other magicals can go there. You'll learn all this, don't worry."

I gulped. I sure hoped I would. I felt so left out.

"Let's get to the pond!" Skeeter said and clapped his hands together. "I've got a Dungeons and Dragons game at midnight and I do *not* want to miss it."

In the back garden we all stood around and watched while Skeeter unpacked various magical trinkets from his backpack.

"This will take a bit of time," the racoon said as he looked back to see us all playing audience. "So maybe y'all can… skedaddle and stare at something else while I work. I'll come back into the house when I'm done."

Back inside Artemis cornered Lizzy to fetch some of his toys from a box in the attic.

"This better not be a trick," she said as she followed the cat up the stairs. "Want to come Chelsea?"

"I'll have a look around the rest of the house, but I'm steering clear of the attic."

I explored and had a good look around and got to know the house's layout. As you entered the house there was the hallway, with a staircase leading up to the second floor. To the left of the hall was the lounge, and on the right, there was the kitchen, which ran the entire length of the house to the back wall. The lounge led through to a dining room located in the back-left corner of the house, which also joined up with the kitchen.

A small utility room was underneath the stairs, and a set of stairs led down into a basement. Another room I would not be exploring.

The next two floors both had two bedrooms and a bathroom.

There was a small study on the second floor, and on the third floor there was a locked door that I couldn't access. On the landing of the third floor the attic door was open, and light shone down as I heard Lizzy and Artemis arguing about which box she was supposed to be reaching for.

Turning around I saw Adam on the stairs below me. I jumped slightly.

"Sorry, I didn't mean to scare you. There are maintenance troubles in the house that I want to go through with you," he said. "Can I run them by you really quick?"

"Uh… I'll be honest, Adam," I said as I passed him on the stair and made my way back downstairs to the kitchen. He followed me as I went. "I'm not really planning on sticking around here long. I'm only visiting the island for two weeks and then I go back to the mainland, I've got to worry about getting a job or I'll be homeless."

I started looking through cupboards in the kitchen. I wasn't sure what I was looking for, but I was nosy and wanted to poke around. There were old tins and out of date items mostly.

"Maybe I don't understand," Adam said, clearly intent on following me everywhere. "You have a home here now. Why would you leave this to be homeless somewhere else?"

"I inherited the house because of a loophole. I was never meant to get this place. My plan is to divide it up amongst the family. If I get a bit of money out of that then it's a blessing." I opened a cupboard over the cooker, and the door came completely off its hinges. "I can't live in this place."

"It's a beautiful house, it just needs a little tender loving care."

"Perhaps our definitions of a 'little' differ." I moved into the dining room to inspect it. Like the rest of the house it was dust-riddled and dreary.

"There's a problem with the pipes," Adam said. "That's first on my list. The pressure has dropped in the last few weeks and I can't figure it out. I just want you to know I'm working on it. Griselda's fridge keeps providing bottles of water. Must be something to do with the house's magic."

"I had noticed the water problem." The kitchen sink had drenched Lizzy the other day when she tried to fill the kettle. "It's an old house. The pipes are probably rusted to bits."

Adam shook his head. "No. The water would be a coppery color if that was the case."

"Okay…"

"The roof needs retiling. I might be able to get it done before my contract expires, I'll need supplies though."

"Um… you might be best taking this stuff up with Lizzy. I dare say the family will want the house repairing if we sell, but I haven't got the money to pay you for all these repairs."

"Well Griselda provided me with a small maintenance budget in my contract, on top of my wages. It was to cover any repairs that might need doing."

I paused. "If she gave you the money then why are you running this stuff by me?"

"I wanted to make sure you were happy with the plans. Griselda was happy enough to let me get on with my work, but you might want to be more involved."

"I appreciate your diligence, but I'm happy for you to work however you like. You don't have to come to me for permission."

"Easier to beg for forgiveness, right?" He chuckled.

I smiled at the behemoth mountain man. His flannel shirt was rolled up at the sleeves, exposing forearms that were corded with thick muscle. He had to be at least six foot five, and with his sheer size I'd put him at over two hundred pounds. He might just have been the largest person I'd ever seen, but he was the epitome of a gentle giant.

"You worked for Griselda, that means you saw more of her than most people did. Did you notice anything unusual in the days leading up to her death?"

His dark brown eyes focused as he considered the question.

"She seemed jumpier than usual, but she was still cordial. A lot of people said things about Miss Griselda, but I never had a problem with her."

"I am the greatest wizard alive!" Skeeter boomed proudly as he scurried through the back door of the house. In one hand he had a VHS cassette.

"You did it?!" I said in excitement. I paused at seeing the tape. "What it is with this town and VHS?"

"Pendle is a little behind the times," Adam smiled. "We only got DVD a few years ago, but I still prefer tape."

"It's the superior format," the racoon nodded as he threw the tape to me. "Now if you don't mind, I'd like you to take me home. I've got goblins to slay and my party doesn't like to wait."

With renewed hope I turned the tape over in my hand and felt as though we were finally making progress. We had the evidence Deacon wanted.

10

The next day Lizzy and I ran the tape over to Deacon, after Lizzy's fresh strawberry pastries of course. He wasn't happy to see us at first, but his attitude changed quickly upon seeing the tape.

"Who is Artemis?" he asked.

"That's her cat. She liked to leave messages for him," I said.

Deacon raised a suspecting brow. "And what's this part about 'warning other witches.' What does that mean?"

"Griselda was one of those pagan types." Lizzy rolled her eyes and tutted. "Crystals, chakras, cleansing auras… all that kind of nonsense. You know the type."

He tapped his fingers over his desk. "I'm not sure about this."

"What's wrong?" Lizzy and I glanced at one another.

"An old woman leaves messages to her cat and thinks she's a witch. It raises some questions about her mental faculties. If her mind was on its way out, then I would expect some paranoia and delusion."

"She wasn't bonkers, Deacon," Lizzy stressed. "She was just eccentric. Come on. You asked us for the evidence, and we brought it to you. Isn't this what you wanted?"

"I guess you're right," he said after a long moment. "Something tells me this is worth looking at."

"You'll take it to the judge?" I asked excitedly.

"Sure will," he said. He turned out of his chair and grabbed his jacket. "I'm going to run this down to townhall now. Judge Barrow is there until noon. If I hurry, I can get the ball rolling."

I was pleased to see Deacon was taking this thing seriously now.

"What should we do?" I asked.

"It's probably best you both tag along. If Judge Barrow has any questions about the case, you can provide more info." He glowered at Lizzy. "Wait a second. Are you allowed near the town hall?"

"Not for another month," she beamed proudly. "I'll have to hang back on this one." She looked at me. "I've got some outfit shopping to do. Meet me at Ali Baba's after lunch?"

"Ali Baba's?"

"It's the fancy-dress shop in town. There's a big Halloween fair at the end of the month and the whole town dresses up. We can pick out outfits together."

Deacon led the way out of the station. I was excited to take a ride in a cruiser, but he walked past the line of police vehicles parked outside.

"I thought we'd be speeding through traffic with sirens on," I said sadly.

Deacon laughed and pointed across the park to a large columned building on the other side. "The townhall is only a minute's walk that way. I tell all the guys to walk over if they have to visit. Walking is good for you and it saves the planet from more exhaust fumes."

I swooned. An environmentalist. A man after my own heart.

"Do you think this judge will sign off on the exhumation?"

"I hope so. We don't get a lot of bad action in this town, so the thought that a murderer is on the loose is quite worrying."

"What did Lizzy do to get barred from the townhall?"

We crossed the road on the opposite side of the park and started up the tall steps leading into the townhall. Deacon pointed at dried red paint that was splattered across the entrance.

"She did that. They've been trying to scrub the stuff off for a month and they've had no luck. The council sold off part of the island recently to a company that tests drugs on animals. A lot of people showed up to protest the move, and Lizzy was at its forefront. The protest was mostly peaceful until she pulled the paint out. She covered our council head from head to toe. He has a restraining order against her for three months."

My cousin the activist.

"I had no idea."

Inside Deacon approached the welcome desk where a receptionist called through to Judge Barrow's office to see if he was available. Once we had the go ahead, I followed Deacon down the spacious marbled hallway to an office with heavy wooden doors and a golden plaque.

"Come in!" a graveled Scottish voice said from inside.

Judge Barrow was a large red-faced man with tiny round glasses. He had short silver hair and thick white brows.

"How about those cowboys last night?" he said to Deacon.

"Appalling," Deacon groaned. "I'm considering changing teams."

"And who are you?" Barrow said. He was the type of person that shouted instead of talking, but he seemed friendly enough.

"Chelsea Moon. I'm visiting the island. I inherited Griselda Sponks house."

Barrow withdrew his hand sharply and mock fear spread over his face. "Oh dear. You're not going to cover me in paint, are you? You Sponks women have a reputation!"

I smiled and rolled my eyes. "I won't but my cousin might if you had anything to do with this animal testing plant."

Barrow scoffed loudly and sank back into his leather chair. "Do I look like a nitwit? I voted against it! Fear ye not, Miss Moon, you might think me a pig in a silver wig, but I'm one of the good guys, or at least I try to be."

"Barrow is my preferred judge because he's easy to deal with," Deacon said. "There are two other judges on Pendle council and they're not as amiable."

"Stop, you're making me blush!" he shouted. "I guess this is the tape you were talking about, aye? Whack it in the VCR and let's watch then."

Deacon walked across the room to a TV in the corner and inserted the tape. I was surprised a VCR player was so readily available, but by the sounds of it the entire island was living in the past. He pressed play and the message started. It was only short, but Barrow watched it a couple of times. After the third play through he looked at me.

"Artemis?" he asked.

"That's her cat."

"Witches?"

"She's pagan," I said, mirroring Lizzy's earlier lies to Deacon. Barrow nodded as though the answers made sense. He didn't seem concerned about the odd details as Deacon had been.

"So, you suspect foul play?" he asked me.

"Wouldn't you?" I kept his eye. I got the sense that Barrow *was* one of the good guys, but I also got the impression he was trying to get a read on me. He shrugged.

"People get senile as they grow old. Maybe she was paranoid, but something tells me it might be worth checking out." He looked at Deacon. "What do you want?"

"An order for exhumation and an autopsy. If there's a murderer on the loose then we need to do something about it."

Judge Barrow thought about the request for a long hard moment and then nodded.

"I'll sign your order, but I don't want this spreading out about town. There's enough on my plate at the moment, and the last thing I need is for this to be in the papers. Complete confidentiality," he said. "Clear?"

"Clear," Deacon repeated.

"Clear!" I shouted. We were making progress. I was excited.

"While I've got you here Deacon, I'd like to quickly go over the station budget for the next quarter. There are some errors on the paperwork that need correcting. It will only take two minutes." He looked at me. "Miss Sponks, would you mind waiting outside?"

I excused myself and closed the door behind me while Deacon and Barrow conducted their business in private. I wondered aimlessly down the corridor until I heard an argument through an open office door only a few feet away.

I knew I shouldn't pry, but something pulled me forward.

"I don't care! You either make up the difference or find a job somewhere else! I'm sick of hearing excuses, Francis! Now get out of my office!"

A well-dressed woman hurried out of the open door and shut it behind her. Her straight black hair was pulled back in a bun. She looked stern but upset. She wiped away tears from her eyes and nearly walked straight into me.

"Get out of the way!" she snapped as I jumped to the side. Her heels clacked quickly along the hallway and then she was gone. A minute later Deacon was back with me.

"You look like you've seen a ghost," he said.

"I nearly just got runover by a small angry woman." I looked at Deacon. "What's the news with the exhumation?"

"Barrow is on it. He's wants the autopsy done and dusted by this evening."

"That's surprisingly fast. I thought bureaucracy took forever."

"Usually it does, but in cases like this time is of the essence. Crucial evidence might decay if we wait." He looked down at his watch. "Well I'm hungry. Want to get lunch with me?"

"I—" I paused. I kind of did actually. I wanted to talk with Deacon more about Griselda's case and maybe even talk with him about other things. Like, how did he get his moustache so neat? Why was I so into it? How were his eyes so bright?

"You're thinking of a polite way to say no."

"It's not that, it's just that I'm meant to visit Lizzy at this dress up shop. Could you give me a ride? Maybe we compromise and get drive-thru on the way?"

"You got a deal Miss Moon. I take it you've not tried Jungle Burger yet?"

Twenty minutes later we were sat in the parking lot of Jungle

Burger, and I was finishing the last of my Mega Jungle Meal. I polished off the last fry and sighed happily to myself.

"The food on this island is something else altogether," I said to Deacon. "I haven't eaten a bad meal since I got here."

"We are a town of food lovers," he said proudly. "You should really try as many of the different joints as possible before you leave. How long did you say you were here for?"

"I was planning on staying two weeks," I said. "But if all the food is this good, I might have to add on more time."

"Well I sure hope you do," Deacon said, his bright green eyes burning into mine. It suddenly felt very hot in the car.

"You do?" I gulped.

"Oh sure. It's always nice to see a new face in town, and another Sponks woman is sure to keep things interesting." He put the cruiser into gear but hesitated before pulling off. "That was a joke, you know that right? If you start acting like your cousin, I won't hesitate to put you into handcuffs."

Handcuffs? *Meow!*

A short car ride later Deacon dropped me off outside Ali Baba's. "Thanks for lunch," I said.

"Thanks for the company. Where are you staying at the moment? The house up on Cherry Road?"

I shook my head. "I'm staying with Lizzy at the moment. The house is a little grim."

"Well I've got your number. I'll give you a call when we get an update on the autopsy. Fingers crossed it comes back clear. The last thing we want is a killer on this rock."

Deacon pulled off and I caught myself wondering what his day would look like from here. Did he have a girlfriend he might visit? Would he be rescuing cats from trees? Foiling bank heists? Filling out paperwork and sighing?

I looked up at Ali Baba's, a large warehouse unit in the middle of a wide tarmac parking lot. The front of the shop had been decorated to look like a cave entrance. It was quite a sunny day, and outside the shopfront a woman was dressing mannequins in various fancy-dress costumes. She looked up at me and smiled as I approached the door. She had thick black eyeliner, pastel pink hair and a face wrinkled from years of laughter.

"Howdy! I'm Angel!" she said with a friendly wave. "Are you new in town?"

"Sort of. I'm visiting family. Your husband doesn't happen to be a pilot, does he?"

"You know my Smithy?!"

"He flew me in the other day. My name is Chelsea Sp- Chelsea Moon. He had a truck full of your mannequins."

"Oh Chelsea *Sponks.* Smithy told me all about you! Well I'm glad to meet you darling. Now do me a favor and give me a hand with Aladdin would you? I need to hoist him up there. He's going to be punching Cinderella in the face."

Before I could say anything, Angel dumped the mannequin into my arms. She climbed up a stepladder propped against the wall and we struggled with fixing the dummy against the wall. After a few minutes' worth of fighting Angel stepped down from the ladder and clapped her hands.

"This," she said while moving her hands across the storefront, "is my Sistine Chapel. I'm going to have a bunch of mannequins in uniforms all across the storefront, all in various poses. You think I'd make the paper?"

"You might even go viral," I said optimistically. I couldn't quite see what she was picturing, but in my mind, I was seeing a bar brawl crossed with a nativity scene.

Inside the shop was a treasure trove of tall aisles, all filled to the brim with hundreds of different fancy dress costumes. Quite a few townsfolk were milling about the aisles. I didn't have to look very hard to find Lizzy. She was behind the front desk.

"Are you supposed to be there?" I said.

"Of course I am, what do you think I am, some sort of delinquent?"

"Deacon told me why you are barred from townhall."

She laughed. "Do you think I was out of line?"

"No, I guess I agree actually. Do you work here?"

"No. I help out Angel sometimes when she needs a hand. I'm just watching the till while she constructs her scene outside." She dipped under the desk hatch as Angel reentered the shop.

"Thanks darling!"

"No problem, cupcake! So, how was the townhall?" Lizzy said to me as we wandered through the shop.

"Good, the autopsy happens tonight. Deacon is going to call me when the results come in."

"Tonight?" Lizzy turned grey.

"Yeah, what's wrong with that?"

"It barely gives us anytime at all. We need to be there, for the exhumation at least. We have to stop Griselda's spirit from attacking the mortals."

I gulped. "I didn't realize that was going to be a problem."

"It is, and I'm going to need at least two other witches with me to help keep her spirit under control."

"I could help."

"No offense Chelsea but this involves pretty advanced magic and I'd be putting you in real danger by asking you to step up on your own. I'll have to call around the family and see if anyone is willing to assist us."

We rushed out of Ali Baba's as Lizzy started rapidly dialing various people in her contacts list.

"I don't understand, what's the worst could happen?!" I shouted as I ran after her through the lot.

"Someone could get hurt!" she shouted back to me. "Or worse. Killed!"

11

The graveyard looked drastically different under the spooky yellow moonlight. A chill was in the air. Mists rolled over the grass and swirled round the many gravestones. We were hiding in a spiky bush about fifteen feet away from Griselda's grave.

Lizzy had managed to recruit the two other witches she needed to make sure we could keep Griselda's ghost held back. There was Glenda, one of my many unknown aunts, and Rosalind Faust, a young woman from another witch family in town.

Glenda was a large woman with ruddy cheeks, a pervasive smile, and a little button nose. Though Lizzy had asked the gang to dress appropriately for the mission Glenda had turned up wearing a pink cardigan, a floral dress and she was actively knitting. She continued despite the loud shushing from my cousin.

"Want a humbug, Chelsea?" Glenda said as she popped one of the sweets into her mouth.

"Ooh, yeah. Go on then!" I said eagerly. Glenda passed one of the sweets back and I fussed with the noisy plastic wrapping.

"Where's my humbug?" Rosalind asked from behind us.

Glenda hadn't taken Lizzy's dress code seriously, but Rosalind had. She was dressed in black from head to toe and had even taken to applying camouflage paint. Her commitment to the role was only made more amusing when I learned she was a dog walker.

"In the bag with your manners," Glenda said. Her little hands didn't miss a beat of knitting.

Rosalind sighed. "Can I *please* have a humbug?"

"It's *'May I'*, Rosalind, "but yes, you *may.*"

Glenda passed back the humbug.

Lizzy was squat at the front of the group with binoculars pressed up against her eyes. She lowered them and looked back at us. "Can you guys please try and take this seriously? Stop snacking, stop knitting, and stop making so much noise!"

"Oh relax, we've got our bubble of silence!" Glenda said pleasantly.

"That won't stop them from seeing a bush moving strangely, will it?!"

"There's no need to be so stressed out dear," Glenda soothed. "You're acting like this is my first exhumation."

Rosalind, Lizzy and I all looked at one another.

"What do you mean, this isn't your first exhumation?" Rosalind asked.

Glenda chuckled to herself. "You girls. This is a cakewalk, trust me, I've done this all before. Hopefully I won't have to stab anyone this time."

Lizzy and I locked eyes. I shuffled away from Glenda ever so slightly.

Mental note. Glenda is crazy. Do not mess with Glenda.

"Shh!" Rosalind hushed. "I see light!"

Silence lapsed over the group and we sat with bated breath, watching as Deacon approached Griselda's grave with two other men. I noticed a small clicking sound and looked over to see that Glenda was still knitting. Deacon and the men talked momentarily and then one of them, a man in a blue boiler suit, disappeared and returned a minute later with a small digger.

They started digging the grave.

"Okay," Lizzy said as she turned back to the group. "They're going to realize very quickly there's a slab of Pendle slate between the earth and the coffin, but once that's out the way they'll haul the coffin up. Once they set it on the ground anything could happen. Griselda might not wake up at all, but if she does, we need to act."

We kept on watching. Sure enough the digger hit the slab very quickly. The men exchanged confused shrugs with one another and then the undertaker moved the slab out of the way with the digger's scoop. He kept on digging.

"What do we do?" I asked nervously. I had never been in a magical situation like this before and still didn't know a *thing* about magic. How was I supposed to be helpful?

"A few things," Lizzy said. "Most important of all we need to charm the men to see something else. If Griselda's ghost bursts out and attacks them, we need an illusion."

"I can put the idea of a wild bobcat in their minds," Rosalind offered.

"Perfect!" Lizzy said. "Can you do it now?"

Rosalind closed her eyes and a gentle wind fluttered out all around us. I felt a change in the air and then heard a roar in the distance. Deacon and the other men all turned around and froze.

"Hurry up!" Deacon shouted to the man working the digger. "I don't want to deal with a hungry bobcat!"

"What else?" I asked.

"Protection," Lizzy said. "Glenda and I will take care of that."

"What about me? I know I'm a magical noob, but I want to help."

"You can help," she said with encouragement. She pulled out a container of table salt and handed it to me. "Here, take this."

"What do I do with this?"

"When Glenda and I pin Griselda's ghost down you draw a salt circle. I also need you to shout her name to keep her attention away from the men. Using a thing's real name is the most effective way to control—"

"Showtime!" Glenda shouted. I looked back to the exhumation to see the coffin had touched the ground. As soon as it did the lid burst open and a turquoise blue figure roared out of the box and went straight for the men.

Glenda and Lizzy were on their feet before I could even react. Their hands were raised, and powerful beams of red light were shooting out.

"Bobcat!" Deacon shouted. "Run, run!"

The three men fled from the scene, which gave us time to deal with Griselda.

"Go!" Rosalind shouted to me; her eyes clouded over with white. "The men won't see us because of my illusion!"

I jumped out of the bush and ran after Glenda and Lizzy. Glenda held one hand above her, red light scorching from her palm into the sky as she aimed at Griselda. In her other hand she had a chocolate bar.

"Really, Glenda?!" Lizzy shouted. Both her hands were focused on Griselda. She saw me. "Chelsea, shout her name, come on!"

Right. I'd forgot about that.

"Griselda!" I shouted. The thundering blue spirit suddenly paused and turned it's glowing white eyes on me. Uh-oh.

"Keep shouting, darling!" Glenda said between mouthfuls of chocolate bar. "Draw salt behind you as you run!"

Run?

The spirit divebombed at me, and then I realized that I was the bait in Lizzy's plan. I held the saltshaker out behind me and started sprinting while I shouted Griselda's name over and over again.

In all the chaos and calamity, the plan somehow worked. After sprinting around Griselda's open grave half a dozen times, I had managed to draw salt circles that had gotten consistently smaller until the final one was small enough to surround Griselda in a tight loop.

Glenda and Lizzy stopped firing red light and both approached the spirit banging on the invisible walls of the salt circle. She looked furious.

"How's the afterlife, Aunt Griselda?" Glenda said. "We all miss you very dearly." Griselda's ghost looked like it was screaming profanities against her salt prison. Glenda merely shrugged and pulled out a glass jar. "That's nice, sweetie. Want to stay in here for a bit?"

With a flash of white light, the blue spirit zoomed into the jar. Glenda closed it again and slipped it back into her large handbag.

"Nice job," Lizzy said to us both. "You especially, Chelsea. You did really well considering this is your first brush with real magic."

"They're coming back!" Rosalind shouted from beside the bush. "The illusion is breaking apart!"

We all fled from the grave and ran back to the bush. Deacon and his compatriots returned.

"Damn thing came out of nowhere!" Deacon said. "Oh well. Looks like it's gone now. Let's get the coffin over to Hank and he can start the autopsy. The sooner we have results the better."

When the men had gone, we crept back out of the graveyard and back to Lizzy's car. We drove Rosalind and Glenda back home and decided to get a late-night shake at Aztec Pancake.

"Huh, I have like five missed calls from your lawyer guy," Lizzy said as we sat down to our table.

Jack?

"Oh… fudge. I was supposed to go out to dinner with him tonight. I completely forgot!"

Lizzy's mouth dropped. "You stood him up! Damn! You go Chelsea. Treat them mean, keep them keen!"

I sank into my chair. I felt like I could die. How had I forgot about the date? I could only imagine how embarrassed Jack must have felt waiting in the restaurant by himself.

"I'm a terrible person. I can't believe I'd do this to another person. Am I really turning into my mother?"

Lorelai Moon. The maneater. Was I inheriting that too?

"Oh, don't beat yourself up. It's not like you didn't have a reason. If this guy really likes you, he'll let you make it up to him. If not, c'est la vie. There are plenty of other fish in the sea." Her phone started buzzing across the table. "Speaking of, there's another one calling now. For you, I presume."

She pushed the phone across to me and I saw Deacon's name on the screen. A flash of relief washed through me. I wasn't sure I could face Jack right now.

"Deacon? Is everything okay? How was the exhumation?"

"It was, uh, eventful. We got attacked by a bobcat, but we managed to get Griselda out of the ground without anyone getting hurt. I'm calling about the autopsy. Hank's had a quick look at the body and he's already given me an answer."

"Oh, that was fast."

"Lucky, I think. Hank happens to be one of the country's leading medical toxicologists. This particular case falls right within his specialty."

"What does that mean?"

"She was poisoned, Chelsea. Your great aunt Griselda was murdered."

1 2

The next day Deacon swung by the house to pick me up and take me to the station. Now it was clear this was an official murder investigation he wanted to speak with the family. Lizzy wasn't able to go in the morning; Skeeter had apparently visited her in a dream via means of astral projection. The fat racoon had demanded she settled her debts that morning or she would never get her copy of Jet Ski Zombies 4, which had *just* come in.

"Sleeping Reaper," Deacon said and placed a small sealed bag down onto his desk. Inside was a wiry black mushroom with white dots on its head. "Extremely poisonous. Grows locally on the island. It makes all the blood in the body coagulate until it's too thick to move through the heart."

"How did Hank even know to test for this?" I said in utter disbelief.

He pushed a photo across his table. It was a close up of a pale ear. Tiny black veins flourished across the neck behind it. "Sleeping Reaper causes the blood capillaries to turn black on the surface of the skin, just behind a victim's ears. Hank spotted the distinctive bruising straight away."

"Are we sure it's that? Can't we run a blood test or something?"

"A body is drained of its blood during the embalming process. Hank was able to find trace amounts of the poison in her body. Legally speaking we have all the evidence we need to prove cause of death."

I couldn't believe it. "Someone actually murdered her."

"There's the possibility she ate the mushroom herself. Be it by accident or on purpose—"

"Are you saying you think she killed herself?"

He shook his head. "No. It's my job to offer up all likely scenarios though and make sure I consider all options. As it stands, I think we must assume murder, because of the evidence you and Lizzy provided. There is however one troubling element of the autopsy. Hank couldn't find a trace of the mushroom in her stomach."

I was confused. "Maybe it was digested?"

"No. Hank said this baby is so poisonous it'll kill you within five minutes of eating it. It definitely should have been there."

Well that certainly was puzzling. "What do you think happened then?"

"Motives for murder usually fall into four categories. Lust, Love, Loathing, and Loot."

"You might have to catch me up to speed here, Deacon. I'm not clued in on your police terms."

"Lust refers to an act of passion. Maybe Griselda was embroiled in a heated love triangle and one of her lovers snapped."

"I think we can rule that one out."

"Love usually comes in the form of a mercy killing, though Griselda didn't have a terminal illness, and Hank said that Sleeping Reaper is not a peaceful way to die."

"Scratch that one off then."

"Then there is Loathing. If Griselda had enemies or feuds, they could come back to bite her."

"She might have had a few."

"Lastly is Loot. Did someone kill her for her money and her estate?" His green eyes examined me.

I looked back at him.

"Wait a second. Are you saying I'm a suspect in this?"

Deacon leaned back in his chair and crossed his arms. "I'm going to be unprofessional for a second and tell you the truth. I don't think you did this."

"So why do I feel like I should be sitting here with my lawyer?"

"Because you have to acknowledge the situation is unusual. Your Great Aunt happens to die one week before you return to the island, and you just happen to be the only person that inherits her estate."

"I literally haven't set foot on this island for thirty years!"

"I know that. That's why I don't think you did this. I'm just saying you have to consider how it looks. Maybe you and your cousin worked something out before you flew here."

I felt myself getting hot under the collar. Deacon was right. My coincidental return didn't exactly look good.

"What do you think happened then?"

"I think the only real motive here is Loathing. Loot is off the table for me."

"Why?"

"Griselda first drew up her will twenty years ago, and while she made amendments, she only did so to specify new family members that were exempt from her estate. The records show that she never made a change that would benefit someone, so we can rule out coercion."

"Coercion?"

"Someone wasn't standing behind her with a knife to her neck while she drew up a new will."

"Lizzy said to me that Griselda might be the most hated person on Pendle Island."

"She had her fair share of enemies, that was true, but I can think of other people that might be more infamous."

"Do you have any leads on a suspect?"

He tapped his fingers on the desk. "That is where this conversation has to end."

"What?!"

"This is an ongoing investigation, Chelsea. I can't discuss details with you. I've already said too much."

I opened my mouth to speak but the words fell short. "I—"

"I'll call you if we have any developments, and here." Deacon pulled a cheap cellphone from his drawer and handed it to me. "I got this for you. I'm sick of having to speak with Lizzy every time I want to talk to you. It's got a GoCrow sim. It's the only carrier that works on the island."

I thanked Deacon for the phone, but as I left it felt like the air between us was sullied with something. I barely even knew the man, but I was annoyed that he wouldn't share information with me. I knew this was an ongoing investigation, but Lizzy and I had already been investigating for several days. Surely I was entitled to some information?

From the station I walked a few blocks through town until I had made it to Aesop's Video shop. Inside Lizzy was putting tape after tape through the rewinder.

"How was it?" she said.

I explained what had happened with Deacon and that the meeting had ended on a sour note. Lizzy just smirked. "Figures. He's such a square. I doubt he's ever broken a law in his life. Want to go get tacos after this? Skeeter said he'll write off my debt if I get him a Big Mex meal."

"Actually, I was going to pay Jack a visit and apologize for standing him up last night. Do you mind if I borrow your truck? I'll be back in thirty minutes."

Lizzy agreed. She estimated she'd be rewinding tapes for at least another hour, so it gave me plenty of time to talk with Jack and meet her back at the shop. On the way to Jack's I decided to make a stop and picked up something to aid my apology.

After a short drive across town to the hotel I made my way inside and retraced the route to Jack's office. I knocked on his door and waited.

"Come in," he said.

I opened the door. Jack had stood up, but his face dropped upon seeing me. "Ah. It's you."

"I am sorry I stood you up. It was a really crumby thing to do."

"Well, that's one way to put it."

"If it's any consolation I had a crazy night. They exhumed Griselda and ran an autopsy. They found poison in her blood. The police think it was murder."

The disappointment in Jack's expression faded. "Oh. What? That is crazy."

"Yeah. I'm really sorry I stood you up. I totally forgot about everything else. It was a weird evening to say the least."

He waved a hand dismissively. "Don't worry about that. I completely understand. It sounds like you have a lot on your plate."

"Well I still feel like a jerk about it. I know this doesn't undo the mistake, but I brought lunch. Do you like Jungle Burger?"

Jack's face lit up. "Chelsea Moon that is a mighty fine peace offering. Take a seat. Let's eat."

I joined Jack at his desk, and we ate lunch together. Although I still felt bad about missing our date the air between us quickly lightened, and as we came to the end of the meal, I was laughing hard at one of his courtroom stories.

"That's when the accused burst out *'Your honor she's lying, there was no Rolex in the glove compartment!'* It was pretty obvious after that he *had* stolen his ex's car. I wish all my cases were that easy."

"Criminal law, estate law, council law and a legal rep for a hotel. Are you a swiss army knife lawyer?"

He smiled. "This was back in college. It was one of my very first cases." Jack breathed out and smiled. I felt calm in his presence. He finished the last bite of his burger and cleaned up. "Great lunch. Thanks. I consider us even, Chelsea Moon. Now, I recall you saying something about a problem with the will."

"Right. I think there is a problem. You said that I inherited the estate because I was the only one in the family with a name change. But I'm not the only one."

Jack straightened and immediately turned to his computer. "Oh? Is there someone else?"

"My mother," I said. "Lorelai Moon. We left Pendle together when I was little, and she legally changed both our names to Moon. She should inherit half of the estate."

Jack's brow furrowed as his fingers whirred over his keyboard. "I was sure I'd checked all the records properly," he said. "This stuff is fairly routine. If your mother had changed her name too then—ah. Yeah. Here it is."

He turned the computer screen towards me, there was a legal document upon it. "What's this?" I asked.

"A spreadsheet with DS-11 info. That's the legal department that handles name and title changes. This is your form." My eyes scanned the form. There was only one entry, and it dated back almost thirty years.

Chelsea Rhiannon Sponks to *Chelsea Rhiannon Moon.*

"Pretty simple," I said.

"For you, yes. This is your mother's." He pressed a button and a new spreadsheet appeared. The information went on for five pages. I read through it quickly. Although there was a lot to take in, I couldn't see any name changes.

Mrs. Lorelai Yvette Sponks married *Mr. Jacob Noah Farley.*

Ms. Lorelai Yvette Sponks divorced *Mr. Jacob Noah Farley.*

Mrs. Lorelai Yvette Sponks married *Mr. Ashid Malaq Tarith.*

Ms. Lorelai Yvette Sponks...

And on and on it went.

I couldn't understand. At no point in the document was my mother ever referred to as Lorelai Moon.

"She never changed her name," I gasped.

"No. Not even in all the times she's been married," Jack said. He squinted as though trying to count the marriages.

"Fourteen," I said.

"Fifteen actually." He pointed to an entry at the bottom of the sheet. "She got married again last week."

Mrs. Lorelai Yvette Sponks married *Mr. Nathaniel Edmond Roth.*

"Oh, for goodness sake, mom!" I huffed to myself while shaking my head. "That explains it then. She never changed her name." But why? And why only change mine?

Jack shut his laptop. "She sounds like an… interesting woman."

"I bet you're reconsidering that offer for dinner now," I joked glumly.

He did look sort of terrified.

"I'm not, but I'm leaving you in charge this time. Why not text or call me when you're surer of your schedule."

I gave my new number to Jack. We parted ways and I felt the air had cleared between us. I was going to make it up to Jack properly with a nice night out somewhere in town. I just had to learn where was good first.

Back outside I sat in Lizzy's car as I typed my mother's number into my new phone. It was a call that I had been putting off for weeks, but now it had to be done. She answered after two rings.

"Lorelai speaking, who is it?!"

"Hi mom. It's Chelsea. Have you got a minute?"

13

"*O*h, Chelsea darling! It's so fabulous to hear from you! I'm just about to scuba with Nathaniel. I told you about him, didn't I? Oh, he's lovely. This is the one Chelsea; I can feel it."

"What's your name?" I asked her.

"What?"

"What's your name?" I repeated.

"Lorelai!" She laughed. "Chelsea. Why are you being funny? Do you need money again?"

"I'm back on Pendle Island. You're Lorelai Sponks. Not Moon. You were never Moon. Why?"

Silence breathed down the line.

"Well, bugger," she said grimly.

"Mom? What's going on?"

"Go without me, Nathaniel!" she shouted in the background. "I need to talk my daughter, that's why!" I heard her mumbling to herself as she moved somewhere more private. "Chelsea? Hello dear. Sorry about that. I love that man, but I swear he drives me up the bloody wall sometimes. I wish he was more level-headed like Quincy. Hm. Now I wonder what that silver fox is up to."

"Mom," I said sternly, breaking her from her distraction.

"Ah yes," she sighed. "I guess I have some explaining to do. You're back on Pendle then. I take it you know about the witch stuff?"

"It came up once or twice."

"Jolly good. Here's the thing darling. You and I are not just witches. We're cursed."

"What on earth are you talking about mom? Why would someone curse us?"

"No one cursed us. We were just born with a certain affliction. Some witches draw their magical power differently than others. I draw my magic from love."

"Love?"

"Well, the first part. You know, the exciting bit at the beginning?"

I'd never actually had a serious relationship, or even acted on a crush. Watching mom cartwheel through the country's male population had made me spur any advance that had come that way, not that there had been that many. I had read enough romance books to imagine the feeling though.

"You mean when you're running around giddy, like you are now?"

"Yes darling, the honeymoon period. When I'm in that state of mind my magic is most powerful. Falling in love with another man is the only way I can keep hold of my magic."

"But why did you lie about changing your name? And why did we have to leave Pendle?"

"Our family name is very powerful; without it we wouldn't have access to our powers. If I changed my name, I wouldn't have my magic. And I left Pendle because... well... I'd run out of options. I needed a bigger sea of fish to fry. I needed new men."

"I think I'm going to be sick."

"Darling my magic only comes from falling in love. It has nothing to do with whatever may happen after dark."

"Now I'm definitely going to be sick."

"Chelsea, I don't think you understand. I know you think I'm some crazy maneater that goes around breaking hearts for fun, but I quite literally can't help myself darling. My magic is very taxing on whomever my heart choses. It sucks men in, dries them out and leaves them reeling. Do you think I enjoy living like this?"

"But why do you? What's so bad about staying single and losing your magic?"

"Without magic we wouldn't have survived out here, Chelsea. It was the only thing that kept us going when it was the two of us. I did it to survive."

"You can stop now, mom! I'm a grown woman! You've got money! You've got a nice house! We're not broke anymore!" Well, I was. She wasn't.

She sighed down the phone. "I'm afraid it's not that simple darling. My affliction is so deeply embedded in my soul now that I need to keep feeding it or I will die. This is why I changed your name when you were little."

"You changed my name so my powers wouldn't activate. You didn't want me to be trapped with the curse like you."

My mind was completely blown. This short five-minute phone call had completely flipped my perspective on my mother, our entire life, and her utterly bonkers behavior. She'd done all of this for me. She'd done it all for us.

"I'm sorry. I wish you'd told me all this earlier. All these years I thought you were just a loon."

She laughed. "Oh, we're all loons, darling. That's in the Sponks blood. You have to promise me you'll leave Pendle. Come stay with me and Nathaniel for a bit. I think you'll like this one!"

Now I knew the truth about my mother's tumultuous relationship with love I could only feel sorry for her. "I can't, there are things to do here."

For the first time in a long time we ended up falling into an actual conversation with one another. I told her everything that had happened on the island so far. The most surprising part is that she actually sat there and listened.

"I've got a theory. Do you want to know what I think?"

I sat up. "You know who the killer is?"

"What? No!" The sound of her loud laughter echoed through the phone. "My theory concerning the local wildlife. The sheriff sounds dreamy. The lawyer sounds cute, I bet he's got a wild side. My money is on the groundskeeper. I'm intrigued. What's his secret?"

"Mom are you serious?" I couldn't believe it. I had to laugh, but at the same time I felt another pang of guilt for her. The curse inside her really couldn't turn off.

"Oh honey, what's the harm in gossiping about boys? It sounds like the population has got a fresh set of heartbreakers on the scene. Maybe I should visit the island again!"

"You leave this little island alone. You're happily married now, remember?"

"Eh… I give him three months darling, seriously. He likes country music."

"So do you!"

"Well, yeah, but, he's way too intense about it."

"I'm going to go now; it was good catching up. Thanks for telling me about the curse." Now that I knew about it, I had some decisions to make.

"No problem, and as for Griselda, check in with Kirk and Robert."

"Who?"

"They're the old lunatics that live on either side of Griselda's property. They are both madly in love with her. They've been fighting over her for years."

"How could you possibly know that? No one on the island knows a thing about Griselda's personal life."

"She wrote to me regularly for advice, darling. Everyone knows I'm the one to contact for relationship advice. I had her walking circles around those old loons!"

"Lust… just like Deacon said!"

"I beg your pardon?"

"Mom, I've got to go. I'll speak to you soon!"

Excitement caused my hands to tremble so fiercely that I nearly dropped the phone out the SUV window as I was getting ready to pull off. It looked like another motive was back on the table now, Loathing wasn't the only one.

I had to get back to Lizzy immediately and had to discuss this new theory. My intuition told me that we were about to uncover some real suspects.

Before I put the car into drive, I pulled my phone out again to text Jack. Now I knew about the curse it wasn't a hard decision to cancel our date forever. Maybe I was afflicted like mom, but I didn't have to fall victim to it. I wasn't going to start chewing up men and using them so I could magic up a cup of tea without moving.

Sorry Jack, it's Chelsea. I've been thinking and we should cancel our date. It's nothing personal, I think we're just better off as friends.

Thanks.

I hit send and cringed a little at screwing Jack over again. Little did he know it was actually for the better.

As I slipped into drive, I gripped the wheel tightly and my mind began to whir with possibilities. There was a murder to solve, and something told me that I was the only one that could do it.

14

---

ater that evening Lizzy and I were in her loft. She was playing videogames while I tried to decipher the runes in the Witch's Digest. Although I couldn't read a single word the pages were full of interesting illustrations, and the book was rather fun to look through.

"Oh, your mom is totally telling the truth," she said. "All witches draw their powers in different ways. I've heard of hers before, but it's rare. She's a Wailing Widow."

"None of her husbands have ever died though."

Lizzy looked back at me and shrugged. "It's just a name for a witch archetype. There are dozens of different types, some better than others." She snapped her fingers and another giant book slammed onto the table. I whipped my hand back just in time to avoid getting crushed. This was another copy of Witch's Digest, though this one looked more modern. The design was reminiscent of a magazine from the 80's.

With another snap of Lizzy's fingers, the book flipped open and stopped on a page of mysterious runes.

"What's this?"

"A list of witch archetypes. I don't think a complete list exists, but that'll give you some ideas."

I squinted down at the open page and to my surprise two words popped into English. As soon as they did a block of runes underneath it also changed:

Wailing Widow.

Watch out ladies, this cat's got claws! Lock up your men. The Wailing Widow loves falling in love, and her magic will make quick work of any relationship, no matter how dearly the Widow may love her betrothed!

"I can read it!" I shouted out loud.

"Yay! I knew you'd get it. What came first?"

"I'm reading the bit about the Wailing Widow. It just... popped into English."

"That's how witch runes work. If you learn about something, then its corresponding rune will be legible to you next time you see it. As I just told you about the Wailing Widow, I thought there was a good chance it might help you learn."

"What's your archetype?" I asked.

Lizzy screwed her mouth to one side before answering. "I think it's stupid to put labels on things like magic."

As she said that more runes popped into English on the opposite page.

Punk Monkey

This witch thrives on mischief, mayhem, and chaos. Though her whacky antics might seem intimidating there is usually a noble cause behind her actions. The Punk Monkey is an eclectic but loyal friend.

"Punk Monkey. That's funny. Describes you perfectly."

"Looks like you're picking up runes quickly," she grumbled. "These magazines just make up half this stuff anyway. There's more to me than just mischief. I did get a pretty big magic boost when I threw paint on that councilman though." She laughed.

"I think it's great. I hope my archetype is more benevolent like yours. I don't want to be a heartbreaker like mom."

"Witches usually do take after their mothers, but there's no guarantee you'll be like her. Wailing Widows *are* rare."

"What was Griselda?"

Lizzy paused her game and set down the controller, she came over and looked at the book. "Hm. I'm not sure actually." She traced her finger across pages of runes, which were still mostly illegible to me. One thing I did realize is that random runes were translated in other places. I noticed they were runes from the descriptions I already knew.

"Ah, here we go," Lizzy said. "I'd put my money on this."

She tapped her fingers against a passage, and it transformed into English before my eyes.

Rueful Radish

Angry and prone to argue, the Radish is not a witch to cross paths with. Rage, misery and feuds charge their magic, following the Rueful Radish like a shadow. Though cantankerous and introverted, the Radish is usually a white witch. Little is known about their strange ways, but good luck is said to befall anyone unlucky enough to cross path with a Radish.

Lizzy shut the book and I realized something. "Wait, Griselda was a good witch."

"Well yeah, she was a mean old bat, but she never actively hurt anyone."

"No, I mean, I think Í understand why she was so mean all the time. By being spiteful she knew that good things would befall her victims."

Was she actually trying to be nice to people in her own round-about way?

"Now you've lost me," Lizzy said.

"Take the story you told me about the car dealer."

"John Vance. Right. His dad sold Griselda a car, it ran for twenty years and then she tried to sue him."

"In anyone else's mind that would be insane, but what if Griselda knew different? What if she was somehow thanking John because the car lasted so long? By starting a feud with him..."

"She knew that good luck would befall him!" Lizzy said excitedly.

"Think hard. Did anything good happen to John Vance after his court case with Griselda?"

Stark realization spread across Lizzy's face. "Well yeah, it's funny that you mention it, but he only went and won the lottery. It wasn't a *crazy* amount, but it was enough to buy him some nice things! Do you think that was to do with Griselda's magic?"

I was stunned yet again. Had Griselda been acting like a mean old coot all this time just so everyone else around her could benefit from her good luck?

"Damn," Lizzy said. "I thought Wailing Widow was bad. Griselda spent her life being hated just so other people could prosper."

"This settles it. We have to get to the bottom of her murder. Griselda wasn't going around town starting feuds with people because she was hateful, it was the opposite! If someone killed her there's a good chance it's because Griselda was trying to help them!"

The next morning, we were back at Griselda's house. A very excited Artemis bounded down the stairs to see me, nearly knocking me back as he jumped into my arms.

"Finally! Do you know how dreadful it is listening to that oaf howl all night?"

Adam walked in from the kitchen. His plaid shirt from the day before was torn to shreds and his body was covered in cuts.

"Adam!" I gasped. "What happened? Are you okay?"

"Ah, I'm fine. I fell into a nest of brambles this morning while I was trying to get into the external water tank. I think the reduced system pressure comes from a blockage over there."

"So many... muscles," Lizzy said as she stared at Adam's partly revealed chest. I had to admit it. The guy was jacked.

Maybe mom was right after all?

"Uh, I'm going to go back to my cabin and change," Adam said and promptly exited the room.

"What brings you back here?" Artemis said to us both. "Did you solve the murder yet?"

"No, but we're making headway. Why didn't you tell us Griselda was a Radish? She was trying to help people all along."

"I figured you guys would know that. But yeah, she was a saint. Wait here!" Artemis ran up the stairs and a moment later he returned with a leather journal between his teeth. He dropped it in front of me.

"What's this?" I said as I opened it up.

"She kept track of all her good deeds, she wanted everyone on the island to benefit from her magic in some way. Griselda loved her power. She likened it to playing the villain in a play."

I thumbed through the journal and found story after story.

I was in the StarMart when a little boy ran into me and nearly knocked me down! His mother came up straight away and apologized. I recognized her from around town. She's a single mother with two kids and is struggling. With a little magic the management were soon on my side and banned the woman and her kids from the market. She was so upset! She couldn't afford to shop anywhere else!

The story left a bad taste in my mouth, but then I saw the news clipping on the page next to it.

Local woman on lucky streak!

Things have been tough for Haley French lately, but she's been on a winning streak after landing her dream job as a Senior Artist for world famous designer, Damian Black. If that wasn't enough, we hear that French and Black are set to wed next month after hitting it off!

"Are you seeing this?" I said to Lizzy. Page after page there was a written account from Griselda about a mishap with a local person, and on the page after there was evidence of her luck passing on. "Here's the page about Bob!"

I wanted to read through every story Griselda had left in that journal, but I set it down on the table and refocused. "Artemis, my mother told me that Griselda was embroiled in a love triangle with her two neighbors. Is that true?"

Artemis grimaced. "Yes. She had a heart for both men, though she wasn't always good with Robert."

"Why?" Lizzy asked.

Artemis got us to open the front door, turned around on the porch and nodded at the house number. "Three and a half," he said. "There are quite a few houses on this street, but Griselda's was one of the last ones to be built. It shares a boundary with Number 3, which is Kirk's property, and Number 5, which is Robert's. When this plot was put down it actually reduced his land."

"I don't understand how something like that could happen," I said.

"Juniper Malkin, she was the head witch here at the time. I don't know if you noticed, but there's a crazy pirate ghost steamrolling around this property."

"Oh, I might know him."

"Well Old Mad John was becoming a problem. His spirit is so engrained here that he's impossible to remove, and Juniper decided a witch needed to live on the road to help contain him. With a bit of magic, she had a house built between two existing plots."

"I can see why that might have angered the neighbors," Lizzy said, "but the plots up here are massive. They can't really be that mad about losing a little bit of land for one house?"

"The problem," Artemis said, "is that Robert's mother was buried at the bottom of his land. When Griselda's house was built it meant his mother was now on her land."

"Ah…" I said with glum realization. For anyone else that wouldn't have been a problem, but I knew with Griselda things would be different.

"Yeah," Artemis said. "She was very open with him. She said he could visit the grave whenever he wanted, but he was still unhappy about it. Things soured between them recently when Griselda blocked him from accessing her land completely."

"Why would she do that?" Lizzy said to me.

"I think it's time we found out."

15

The gate at the bottom of Robert's drive was a lot fancier than Griselda's. His driveway was paved, and the gate was connected to a keypad. We buzzed the intercom.

"Not interested!" a grizzly old voice snapped. "Go away!"

"Time for Punk Monkey to shine," Lizzy said. She pressed her finger against the keypad and a spark of electricity zapped across the metal keys. The gate opened and Lizzy drove up the driveway. "Hopefully he doesn't have a gun."

We pulled up in front of a large and expensive-looking lodge. As we stepped out of Lizzy's SUV an old man in a bathrobe came hurtling out the front door with a rifle in his hands.

"How the?! You have ten seconds to get off my property!" Robert said, aiming the rifle square at us.

"Calm down, you old coot," Lizzy sighed. With a snap of her fingers Robert's rifle twisted itself into a pretzel shape. He stared at the gun in surprise and then at us.

"Witches."

"I figured you'd already know about our kind as you spent most of your life in love with our Great Aunt Griselda. Please correct me if

I'm wrong and I'll wipe your memory." Lizzy kept her hands pointed at him.

Robert scowled at us but lowered his now useless gun. He turned around and walked back inside his house.

"Where are you going?" I shouted.

"We talk inside. It's too cold out here!"

Lizzy and I looked at one another and followed Robert inside his house. The interior was rustic, blending stone with wood for a cozy and authentic feeling. I had no idea how much a property like this would be worth, but I could tell it was a lot.

Robert led us into a large designer kitchen and boiled the kettle. "Tea? Coffee? Whiskey?"

A few minutes later we were sat around a long oak table.

"Why are you here?" he said tiredly.

"It's about Griselda. She was murdered. We were wondering if you might know anything about it."

"Nope."

"You seem awfully calm to have just learned she was murdered."

Robert took a sip of his coffee before answering. "I already talked to the police. I don't know why I have to explain myself all over again, especially to a couple girls breaking and entering."

"The police were here?" Lizzy asked.

He nodded. "Apparently I'm a suspect. They got wind of me and Griselda falling out."

"Was this about your mother's grave?"

"Sure was. I know Griselda liked to go around causing trouble with other folk. Can't say I understood why, but that's part of the reason I loved her. She kept things interesting."

"You never had a problem with her though?"

"No. She was one of my closest friends. But things changed leading up to her death. She was acting all paranoid. She started acting cold towards me. Very cold."

"How so?"

"Told me she didn't want to see me anymore. Said she was choosing him over me."

"Him?"

"That idiot down the road. Kirk." He clenched his jaw. "Griselda had a big heart. She loved both of us. Can't say I liked it, but she made it clear to us both she wouldn't pick. Well that finally changed. As if that wasn't enough, she got a restraining order against me. She even said I couldn't visit my mother's grave anymore. Said she'd called the police and report me for trespassing. Griselda cut all her ties with me."

"That kind of harsh treatment would definitely give you motive to kill her," Lizzy said bluntly.

Robert rolled his eyes and looked at her. "I didn't kill the only woman I ever loved. I was at the community theatre that night, helping out with the latest school production. People have already vouched for me." He pushed his chair back from the table and stood up. "Now if you excuse me, I actually have stuff to do today. I'll send you a bill for the gun and the keypad."

Lizzy snapped her fingers again and the gun untied itself on the kitchen table. "Already sorted."

"Just get off my property," he growled.

As we were on the porch stairs I stopped and looked back at Robert. "I don't know if I made this clear, but I inherited Griselda's estate. I'm your new neighbor now."

"Oh, goody."

"I'd like to make a peace offering," I said. "Let's redraw the boundary lines. I want you to have your mother's grave back." Robert only glared back at me. "We'll err... figure the details out another time!"

"Why did you do that?" Lizzy asked as we pulled away in her car.

I shrugged. "If he's going to be my neighbor I might as well try and make peace."

"So you've decided you're staying," Lizzy said with a smile.

"I—" I paused. It hadn't even really occurred to me. "Maybe."

"I think we need to tell Robert the truth," Lizzy said. "Griselda obviously did all that horrible stuff because she knew she was going to die. By cutting ties with Robert she made sure something good would happen to him after she was gone."

"If Griselda cut ties to reward Robert with her magic, then that means she already suspected someone else of trying to murder her."

"It doesn't rule him out though," Lizzy said. "Even with his alibi. Griselda was poisoned. He could have arranged that before he left for the evening."

It still didn't explain why there was no mushroom in Griselda's stomach. It still didn't explain a lot of things.

"Let's go see what Kirk has to say."

Just how vicious was this love triangle?

***

Down the road we found Kirk's place, which was the antithesis of Robert's. There was no gate at the bottom of his drive, there were dogs everywhere and his house was a large…

"Watch out for the dogs, they'll cover you in drool!"

"Is that a… Tipi?" Lizzy said as we climbed out of her car.

"I prefer the term yurt," Kirk said. He was walking towards us. "Welcome to Kirk's yurt!" He laughed. "Just a little joke I have with myself. Are you dropping off dogs? I'm technically fully booked at the moment, but they can sleep in the yurt with me."

"Dogs?" I asked and looked around. There had to be forty dogs here and they were running around everywhere.

"You're looking at Kirk's Dog Kennels. I look after dogs for people. The kennels are at the bottom of my property, but I let the dogs run free in the day. They love it up here. Do you want some ginseng tea?"

"We just had drinks. We also don't have a dog," I said. "We just came here from Robert's place."

Kirk had a face full of laughter lines and a long silver ponytail. He was a hippy from head to toe, but his jovial manner dissolved as soon as we mentioned Robert.

"I don't believe I got your names," he said shortly.

Lizzy and I introduced ourselves. "I just inherited Griselda's place,"

I said. "I thought it would be nice to introduce myself to the neighbors."

"Ah! I see. Word of warning then as you're new. Take heed of Robert Lachlan. The man's bad news all around."

"Is that why Griselda chose you over him?"

Kirk's expression faltered. "I'm a little confused. What exactly was the nature of this call? This isn't the 'borrow a cup of sugar' conversation I was expecting."

"I'm sure you've heard by now that Griselda was murdered. Did the police talk to you?"

He stiffened. "They did." Kirk looked around at his dogs, who were running about all over the place. "They've got this ridiculous idea that I would kill the love of my life just because she chose Robert over me."

Lizzy and I both paused.

"Hang on a second," Lizzy said. "Robert told us she chose you over him."

"I'm just telling you what Griselda told me. She could act in strange ways when she wanted to. That persona she put on around town, that wasn't who she really was."

I was confused momentarily, but I could work out Griselda's reasoning. She had started a feud with both of her love interests so they could both reap the benefits of her luck. A quick glance from Lizzy told me she had worked it out too.

"Maybe she was just sick of both of us," Kirk guessed. "Robert and I were best friends when we were younger. I never thought that coward would have it in him to poison someone."

"What makes you sure it was him?" I asked. "The police seem to think his alibi checks out."

He scoffed. "He's got money. Probably paid them off."

Though I'd only known Deacon a short while something told me he wasn't the type of cop to take bribes.

"What about you?" I said. "You had just as much reason to kill her. It would make you angry thinking Griselda had chosen Robert over you, even if it wasn't true."

"It did make me angry. Truth be told I'm a little relieved to hear it was another one of her strange lies. I wasn't angry enough to kill her though. She's the only woman I've ever loved. Look at his place." He gestured to the overgrown field of grass. Dozens of dogs were still sprinting in all directions. "I was at Woodstock. Do I sound or look like a killer to you?"

"Looks can be deceiving."

"I'm a Buddhist. I don't believe in hurting anyone, regardless of how I feel about them. Besides, I think you're both missing the mark with this Miss Marple routine you're playing."

"What do you mean by that?" Lizzy asked.

"Robert and I hate each other's guts. That's common enough knowledge. Suppose Griselda did choose Robert over me, *and* I was the type of person to fly off the handle in a murderous rage. I wouldn't kill Griselda. I would kill Robert."

"That… makes sense," I said. "In a twisted sort of way."

"And I can guarantee Robert would do the same. He'd kill me, not Griselda." Kirk squinted at us. "Maybe go home and think a little more before accusing anyone else of murder, leave the police to that."

My head was in a whirl as we made our way back to Lizzy's car. From what I could tell Robert and Kirk would both have a motive to kill Griselda (or each other) but at the same time there was no concrete evidence linking either of them to the poisoning.

I noticed something as I climbed into the passenger side of Lizzy's car, however. My eyes wandered to a small cluster of darkness at the base of a tree just feet away from where Lizzy had parked. There were a group of small black mushrooms with white spots on their heads, growing wild on Kirk's property.

Kirk had access to Sleeping Reaper, the same mushroom that had killed Griselda.

couple of days had passed since Lizzy and I had grilled Griselda's two ex-lovers, and in that time all apparent leads had gone cold. Lizzy used the time to help show me around the island, which was admittedly good fun, but all the while my thoughts were focused on Griselda and the fact her murderer was still running loose.

Despite her affinity for mischief, Lizzy did have responsibilities to return to, and the short amount of vacation time she had used to welcome me had now expired. She was back at work at Black Horse Studios, a small set of recording studios that were apparently famous the world over.

"I'm still surprised a place like this exists in Pendle," I said to Lizzy as I dropped her off for her shift. A large biker-type with a red mohawk was behind the reception.

"Lizzy! I need you to start on the masters for Glamour Rat."

"Wow, no rest for the wicked, eh Bash?"

"You've had a week off, what more do you want?!" His eyes turned on me. "And who's this lovely lady?"

"I—"

"This is my *cousin*, Chelsea, and you will treat her with respect. She's not one of the floozies, so go and vulture somewhere else."

Bash acted like he was offended. "I was merely being polite. Stephen's the name, but everyone calls me Bash. Are you sticking around? I can give you a tour of the studio if you're into it. Do you like what I've done with the place?"

"It's pretty cool, I've got to give it to you. I didn't think there would be that many bands on Pendle island."

Bash laughed. "Oh, there aren't. I was treading the waters of bankruptcy for a while before my luck turned around."

"Bash was literally days away from closing when Deerstalker walked through the front door. They wanted to record their next album here. They'd heard a mix he did for a smaller band and liked his sound." Lizzy set her bag on the floor and flicked through some unopened mail.

Now I wasn't the hippest girl in most rooms, but as it went Deerstalker were massive. Their last three albums had been number one for months.

"Deerstalker? Wow, they're like, actually huge!"

Bash smiled. "Too right they are, and since then everyone and their mother has wanted to record an album here. I still can't believe my luck."

I looked at Lizzy momentarily. "Bash, did you ever happen to fall out with my great aunt?"

"That old nut, Griselda?" Bash's eyes widened. "Oh, I did. For sure. I don't know what her problem was. No offense of course. She would file endless noise ordinances against me. She claimed she could hear the racket from our studio all the way up the hill. It was complete nonsense. Eventually I had to file a restraining order against her."

Lizzy and I looked at one another knowingly. "You never told me that," Lizzy said.

Bash shrugged. "She's your family. I didn't want to make it uncomfortable. I tried to be civil with the lady." He looked at both of us. "Sorry for your loss, by the way. How about that tour?"

"Raincheck on that Bash," I said. "I have to go and apologize to my lawyer. Again."

I left Lizzy at the studio and set off in her car to start my own day. A few minutes later I was knocking on Jack Valentine's office door.

"Come in!" he said cheerily. I entered and his face fell. "Oh. It's you."

"I need your help with something, and I figured the swiss army knife of law would be the best person to ask."

"My workload is full, sorry. I can refer you to other lawyers on the island."

"Look if this is about the dinner thing—"

"You're a very rude individual Ms. Moon. Do you know that? One minute you're hot. The next you're cold. Between all your flip-flopping the one thing that doesn't change is that you come to me when you need help with something. All the while there isn't a breath of apology or even a hint of explanation as to what I've done wrong."

"Jack you didn't do anything wrong. My head is just kind of messed up right now. I'm not really in the right place for dating."

He held up his hands in exasperation. "Whatever. What is it you want?"

"You'll help me?"

"I'm the best lawyer on this rock and something tells me you're not going to go away until I help you, so make it quick."

"I really appreciate this," I said with my hands pressed together. "I want to change my name and redraw the boundaries on my land. Could you help me with that?"

Jack swept a hand through his hair. "What on earth are you up to?"

I quickly explained the boundary discrepancy on Griselda's land and how I wanted to give land back to Robert so his mother's grave would be back on his side.

"Sounds simple enough. You'd just need to get your neighbor to agree to the changes. Why the name change though?"

The real answer is that it was the only way I could properly activate my magic. Apparently having the Sponks name was an important part of accessing my powers. As long as I was a Moon, I wouldn't be able to use my magic properly. I couldn't tell Jack that of course.

"I'm thinking of staying here on the island. At least for a while anyway. I'd like to take my original family name back. My mom never changed hers, so… why should I be the sore thumb?"

"A name change is easy enough. I can process the paperwork for you today, but you'll have to go down to townhall to sign some things in person. This won't affect your recently inherited estate by the way, so there's no need to worry about that."

"What about the boundary change?"

"You'll have to speak with domestic zoning down at the townhall. If my memory serves me correctly a woman called Francis takes care of such matters. I believe you'll find her in the council's accounting department."

"Why does an accountant take care of zoning?"

"Everyone down there has multiple hats. They've been over-budget and cutting corners for years. It's a mess really."

"I guess that explains them selling off land to corporations."

"I'll get started on this paperwork for you and have it sent over to the townhall. Now I bill by the hour, and you've only been here ten minutes, but I have to round up, sorry. My hourly fee is $750."

My eyes about popped out my skull. "What?!"

Jack burst into laughter. "Relax. I'm just joking. This one's on the house, but it's my last free favor. The next time you need my help I'll be charging, Chelsea."

I thanked Jack and made my way to the door to leave. Before exiting I turned to him. "I'm afraid of turning into my mother," I said.

"I beg your pardon?"

"That's why I called off the date. I've always been terrified I'll end up like her. You've seen how many times she's been married. I don't want to be that person."

"It was just dinner," he said. "I wasn't going to get down on one knee."

"I just wanted you to know why I was jerking you around. And I apologize, I'm not usually like this. The first time I genuinely forgot, the second time—"

"You were worried I wouldn't have had chance to pick out a suitable engagement ring."

I laughed. "Stop teasing. I just want you to understand what's going on in my head. I'm not messing you around on purpose."

"It's water under the bridge. For what it's worth I'm a child of divorce too. I know what it feels like to grow up around that. I can't imagine what fifteen times feels like."

"Fourteen, she's not canned this one yet," I said. We both smiled.

On the drive to the townhall it felt as though a weight had been lifted off my shoulders. I was glad I'd had a chance to clear the air with Jack, though I still wanted to try and make it up to him somehow. He had been so helpful since I'd arrived on the island, and all I'd done was mess him around in return.

Before I went into the townhall I decided to stop by the police station to try and catch Deacon. I'd been trying to reach him on the phone for days to share my discovery of the mushrooms on Kirk's property, but the sheriff was impossible to get hold of.

"How may I help?" Barbara said from behind the reception.

"I need to speak to Deacon. Is he in?"

"He just went out to lunch."

"It's ten."

"It's an early lunch."

"He's avoiding me."

"Do you want me to take a message?"

I left the station in a huff and was about to make my way over to the townhall when my feet led me down the alleyway behind the back of the police station. There I saw a familiar red-mustached figure creeping out of the back.

"Deacon! Hey! What are you doing?!"

Deacon stared up at me like a deer in the headlights. He froze and then sighed. "You know I thought Lizzy was the biggest nuisance in your family, but I stand corrected."

"You've been avoiding me."

"Yes, but I received your tip. Thanks for the many, *many* messages."

"Kirk has the Sleeping Reaper mushroom on his property, don't you think that's suspicious?"

"The darn thing grows everywhere, Chelsea. I had some in my backyard a few years ago. Am I a suspect now too?"

I fumbled. "Oh, I didn't realize it was that common. Why not just tell me that instead of ignoring me?"

"I have a job to do, which means running around and pursuing active leads. And by the way, I warned you to stay out of the investigation. If I hear you've been running around accusing more people of murder, then you're in trouble."

Trouble? Meow.

"I didn't accuse anyone. I was only speaking to my neighbors! I'm allowed to do that."

"Thin ice, Chelsea. You're on it. If I hear about any more trouble, then I'll come down on you hard. Are we clear?"

I grumbled my response back at Deacon before turning and heading to the townhall.

The name change was surprisingly easy. Jack had already sent all the documents over, like he said he would, and all I had to do was literally sign my name a few times.

"Nearly done," the clerk said. "Now you can pay extra for the change to take effect later today or pay the normal fee and wait a week."

"How much is the extra fee?"

"$75."

"Uh, I'll wait. I've been a Moon all these years. What's another week?"

"Very well. Let's just process this and get your card details." She processed the order. "Done! "Your official documents will come through the mail in the next few days. You will have to update your driver's license and other personal information yourself."

"Thanks! Do you know where I can find a 'Francis'? I need to sort out a boundary discrepancy."

The helpful lady pointed me in the right direction. I followed hallways until a brass plaque reading 'Francis Pitt' identified the right office door. I went to knock but held back my hand when I heard a heated argument inside.

"As far as I'm concerned this is done. If you can't make up the numbers by the end of the week then don't bother coming in on Monday," a male voice said. I heard the sound of footsteps quickly coming my way and narrowly avoided a tall and very-serious looking man.

"Beg your pardon," he said as he marched on his way.

I looked inside the office to see a woman pushing back tears at her desk. It was the same woman that nearly knocked me over the other day. Her expression stiffened upon seeing me.

"Can I help you?"

"I'm looking for a Francis Pitt. I have a boundary discrepancy that needs sorting."

The woman glared at me. "Come in. Shut the door behind you."

I sat down opposite from Francis and couldn't help but notice how uncomfortable the room felt. "My name is—"

"I know who you are," she snapped. "Chelsea *Moon*. You inherited the house up on Cherry Road."

"You know that?" I said with surprise.

"This is a small island, word travels fast. What do you need help with, Miss Moon?"

"It's Sponks now actually, or it will be next week anyway," I said. "I requested a name change back. Felt a bit silly being the odd one out."

Francis raised an eyebrow at my admission. "Oh, really? So, you'll be a Sponks again." Her attention drifted off momentarily before she looked back at me. "That's very interesting."

"Yeah. One week left of being Moon, and then back to my roots. I didn't feel like paying the speedy fee."

Her brow creased and she pulled her monitor towards her. "Well let me see if I can straighten that out for you." Her fingers whirred across the keyboard. "There. I waived the fee. The change will go through later today."

"Oh, wow. That was really kind of you. Thank you. May I ask why?"

"I'm not going to be here much longer, honey." She shrugged. "My head is for the chopping block. The targets around here are ridiculous. If I'm going out, I might as well give out a few freebies. Now, how can I help you with this boundary discrepancy? Would you like a drink?"

"A water if you don't mind."

"Hm," she said with a smirk. "Funny."

"Pardon?"

"Nothing. Let me get that for you."

Using the fountain in the corner of her office she filled us both a glass and then I proceeded to talk her through the boundary request. Francis was able to pull up the property maps on her screen and redraw a provisional border with my input.

"Just here?" she asked.

"No, it's a little further up, this part h—" I lifted my hand to point and knocked my glass of water all over Francis.

"Oh, for goodness sake! My blazer is drenched!" Francis immediately jumped out of her chair and pulled off her blazer. She was wearing a sleeveless blouse underneath.

"Sorry," I said. "It was a mistake. Let me get some paper towels from the…" I paused at seeing her arms. They were covered in scratches. I looked up at Francis. "Are you okay?"

"Kitten," she said with a flippant roll of her eyes. "I got two new kittens the other day and they love to play. Don't worry about the jacket, I can dry it on the radiator. It was an honest mistake. I'll just print off the paperwork you need to sign. You'll need to take a copy over to your neighbor too. There shouldn't be too much trouble as you're surrendering land to him."

She was back a moment later with a stack of thick papers.

"Quite a bit to sign," she said. "But we can get through it fast."

I hated legal work like this. Signing rental contracts always exhausted me and any sort of document requiring a signature always made me suspicious. I felt that way now. A relentless feeling of distrust prickled up and down my spine, but I ignored my old paranoia and quickly signed all the papers. There were a lot.

"Done!" Francis announced cheerily when the last document was signed. "These are the copies you need for your neighbor." She handed over a sliver of papers that were merely a fraction of what I'd signed.

"Seems a lot smaller than my share."

"Bureaucracy. Am I right?!" Francis laughed loudly and stood up to usher me out of her office. "See you around Miss *Sponks*!"

I left the townhall feeling like I'd achieved something. After that I ran the contracts over to Robert, who said he would diligently read through all the paperwork first before signing anything. He seemed happy that I'd put the legwork in though. I don't think he expected me to actually follow through on my word.

It was starting to feel like I was slowly getting settled in Pendle, and when I pulled up at Griselda's house to visit Artemis the strangest thing happened to me as I exited Lizzy's car.

An invisible bolt struck the top of my head and spread through my body like electricity. Tiny sparks danced on my fingertips and the world suddenly seemed like a much bigger place.

I then realized my name change must have gone through, which meant my magic was now in place.

I was a witch. For real!

"Now what?"

*L*izzy text me later that night to say that she had to stay late at the studio to finish an album for an important client. She told me not to worry about the car, Bash would give her a lift to her apartment when she was done.

With a bit of spare time on my hands I decided to hang with Artemis and get to know my familiar a little bit more. I'd mentioned the strange lightning bolt I'd felt outside the house when I'd entered, and we'd been doing a magic crash course ever since.

"Tell me what Mary Malkin said again?" the cat said from the kitchen table.

"Not a lot. She told me to follow my intuition and that the rest would figure itself out. She mentioned that I had something else to figure out first."

Artemis smirked. "Sounds like Malkin all right. She's vague at the best of times, but there is usually wisdom in her words, if you can decipher them. Malkin is quite old school, a lot of witches from her era think the best way to teach is to let someone figure it out by themselves."

"You disagree?"

"I don't see any harm in nudging people in the right direction.

Now you've got your magic I think a gentle push here and there wouldn't hurt. Hold out your hand and face the kitchen door."

I did as the cat said. "Now what?"

"Say the word 'Nitras'. Focus all your energy into it."

I held my hand up and repeated the word, but nothing happened.

Artemis shook his head. "No. Like this." He faced the door. "Nitras."

Plumes of giant flame rippled from Artemis' mouth, making him look like a miniature dragon covered in fur.

"Oh my gosh!" I yelled.

"Neat right? Try again a few more times."

I did as he said, repeating the word over and over to no effect until something actually happened. On the dozenth try a small and pathetic wick of fire dripped from my hand and evaporated on the air. "I did it!" I yelled in excitement. "It was a bit lousy though."

"You'll get better with practice," Artemis said. He took a deep breath and with all his gusto he produced another plume of brilliant golden fire. Unfortunately, Adam happened to be walking through the door at the same moment. The groundskeeper went up in flames.

"What in the!" he roared while spinning around the kitchen to bat the flames out. I grabbed a towel and helped Adam put out the flames. Artemis was on the floor rolling with laughter.

"Are you okay?" I asked as I put the last of the fire out.

"I think I'm all right," he glared at Artemis. "My shirt took the brunt of it."

The fire had made quick work of Adam's plaid shirt, which was now hanging off his body in threads. His back was fully exposed and crisscrossed with long thick scars.

"Adam, oh my… goodness. What happened to your back?"

The groundskeeper turned around to look down at his scars and looked away. "Ah, just old tree surgery scars." He went over to the sink to pour himself a glass of water, but the taps shook and hissed as usual. Adam slapped his hand down. "I keep forgetting about the damn water."

"Here." I got him a cold soda from the fridge. "I'll take a look at the water tank if you like. Maybe small hands can make lighter work of it."

"Give it a go by all means." He knocked the drink back. He would have looked like a model from a commercial, but something was off with his appearance. His skin was starting to look a little grey, and there was a sheen of sweat on his forehead.

"Are you okay?"

Adam looked outside the kitchen window. I followed his eyeline. It was night out now. It was a crisp evening. The moon was white and round, and a serene blue light seemed to shine down on the woods around Griselda's house.

Adam flinched. "I'm not feeling too hot. If it's all right with you I'm going to call it a night and get some sleep in my cabin. I'll see you both tomorrow."

He left so fast there was no time for me to offer a response. I turned around and saw Artemis beaming from ear to ear.

"What's so funny?"

"I should probably just tell you, he's—"

My phone started buzzing in my pocket. As soon as I pulled it out, I saw three missed calls from an unknown number. "Hold that thought kitty. Someone is trying to call me." I called back straight away, but there was no answer. I did get a text a few seconds after that though.

Hey Chelsea, it's me, Jack. There's something I need to talk to you about in private, and urgently. Can you meet me at Hook Point as soon as you get this message?

"Weird. Artemis, do you know what Hook Point is?"

"Yeah, it's where the old mine was before they closed it down. It's a five-minute drive from here."

"What's there now?"

"Bunch of boarded up buildings. I think people go there to make out now." He shrugged. "You got an invitation?"

I bit back a smile. Jack was still flirting with me despite everything that had happened.

"Something like that. Listen I'm going to go out for a bit. If you like I can pick up Chinese on the way back."

"Yes!" he crowed. "Are you staying over tonight?"

"I'll stay late, but I'm not sleeping in this house until I have a new bed. Behave yourself kitty. Be nice to Adam. Don't set fire to him again."

"Eh, we'll see how the evening goes."

I quickly checked my reflection in the mirror before heading out to meet Jack. I couldn't really say why I was indulging this silly little game of his, but I was having a good day and I was excited to see him again. Although I was hesitant to pursue a relationship with anyone, I had to admit I was attracted to the lawyer, and I wanted to hear what he had to say.

With 'Hook Point' set into the GPS I climbed into Lizzy's car and set off. Artemis was right about the close distance, and it only took me five minutes to get there.

The old mine was a wide gravel flat surrounded by boarded up warehouse buildings bordered by dark forest. Driving into the abandoned lot was a little creepy to say the least. It wasn't the make out point I'd imagined.

The weirdest thing is that I couldn't see another car there. Jack's Mercedes wasn't exactly hard to miss. I shut the engine off and climbed out of the car. Just as I did my phone started ringing again. This time Jack's name came up on the screen. He was calling from his phone this time.

"Chelsea, tell me if this is none of my business, but I have a quick question for you. Why did you open up a will today?"

"What?"

"I was finalizing the estate transfer today and had to double check your records to make sure I had all my info right. It says on the file you set up a will today, right after you changed your name and filed for a border discrepancy."

I froze. "I didn't set up a will. What does it say?"

"Well it's another weird one. Is this a trend in your family? The will simply states all your assets and possessions are *nisi heredis.*"

"What does that mean?"

"It's Latin. It basically means your estate doesn't go to any next of kin. It's like a will by exception, but there are no loopholes."

I couldn't make any sense of the situation. "Who does it go to then?"

"Well when an estate isn't contested it will default into the possession of the local governing body. *Nisi Heredis* is basically another way of saying 'give it to the council'."

"Is that why you text me? Are you meeting me at this creepy mine or what?"

He paused. "What are you talking about?"

It was then that I heard footsteps on the gravel behind me. I turned around and saw her.

"Put the phone down," Francis said. I slowly lowered the cell from my ear and dropped it to the ground. It landed face down. Francis laughed to herself. "You have no idea how hard this week has been because of you."

"You killed Griselda."

Francis clapped slowly. "About time someone figured it out."

"She's dead because of you!"

"She was a twisted old bat anyway. And she was stupid enough to spitefully cut everyone from her will. I drew it up for her you know, all those years ago. I've been waiting fifteen years for that coot to die."

I started putting the puzzle pieces together in my mind.

"You wanted her estate to go to the council."

"Things weren't so bad back then; I could afford to wait a little. I thought she had a few years. Maybe three tops. But that crone just kept going."

"You've been under pressure though. The budget is worse than ever."

Francis just laughed. "Well, it's partly my fault. I wanted to get ahead. I made some investment choices with the council's budget and they didn't pan out. Now things are worse than ever, and it's my head on the chopping block. There's a dent in the budget, a big one, and I could only think of one way to make up the hole."

"Griselda's estate. So, you poisoned her. But what happened to the mushroom? There was no evidence in her stomach."

"I was trying to get that stupid crone for weeks, but she kept dodging my attempts. I think she knew someone was after her. Then I had another thought. She doesn't have to eat it. She just has to ingest enough to kill her."

I looked down at Francis's bare arms, which were still covered in scratches. Adam had the same marks after falling from the water tank. "Brambles!" I shouted. "You poisoned the water tank."

"You're a smart cookie," she said with a wry smile. "Smarter than everyone else on this idiot rock. That's why you have to die, Chelsea. You're the only thing that can save my job, and your little detective routine is just winding me up. I'll think up a good suicide letter and give some pathetic reason for you to end your life." She cocked her gun. "Any last requests?"

I held both my hands up. "Wait, wait now! Don't shoot! People won't believe this!"

Francis shrugged. "I haven't really got any options left darling."

Without thinking I flared my hands and shouted 'Nitras!' as loud as I possibly could. The plume that erupted from my hand's still was nowhere near as exciting as Artemis', but this time a reasonable sized tunnel of fire burst five feet in front of me.

"What on earth?!" she roared. Francis stumbled back out of instinct. The fire had barely singed her, but it had given me enough time to turn around and start running. As I ran, I heard her shouting behind me. "Come back here, Moon! We're not done here!"

I'm not the fittest of people. On a good day my idea of exercise is a trip to the fridge to get a bar of chocolate, maybe two trips if I'm feeling adventurous. Hearing the deafening crack of gun pointed at you has a funny way of making you run fast, however.

I bolted sharply around a corner of the nearest boarded up building and heard Francis shouting somewhere in the distance behind me. Two more shots echoed through the night and my chest was starting to burn from the cold night air. I was about to turn another corner when Francis appeared right in front of me. I skidded to a stop and fell onto my knees.

"Don't make any sudden moves!" Francis said as she readjusted her grip on the gun. She was smiling, but there was nothing pleasant about her expression. Her breath was heavy just like mine. "I am *so* done with this. Do you even know what I've done for this town? Without me the council would be nothing. This town would be nothing! This entire island would be a lifeless rock! Years. I've worked years with no thanks!"

"You gambled the council budget on fruitless investments and lost it all. Now you're going to kill someone to save your own job? Please. Spare me the self-pity."

She cocked the trigger back. As she did, I lifted my hand again. "Nitras!"

Francis flinched, but this time nothing happened. I felt an empty frazzle whimper on my fingertips. I must have used all of my meager magic reserves on my previous attempt.

"Looks like your little trick isn't working this time darling. Say goodnight!"

The gunshot rang out through the night, and I closed my eyes as I waited for pain.

My ears were whistling from the gun's loud explosion, and after a few seconds I realized that I was somehow still breathing. Opening my eyes, I saw blinding bright light.

"Heaven?" I whispered to myself.

Then I saw Francis clutching her right knee on the ground. Blue and red halos blurred on the edge of my vision. The bright lights blinding me were the headlights of several police cruisers. Figures rushed forward from the light with guns held out in front of them. Francis was cuffed, pinned to the ground and Miranda rights echoed across the cold night.

Someone ran forward and helped me up to my feet.

"Deacon?" I couldn't understand how they had got here. "How did you—"

"Your lawyer. You didn't end the call when you dropped your phone. He called us from his office, and we traced your phone straight away."

"Recorded the whole thing too," another voice said behind me. Turning I saw Jack standing a few feet away from his Mercedes. "I hit record as soon as you dropped your phone." He looked over at Francis. "Her monologue will make a nice taped confession in court."

Not long after that I was down at the station, wrapped in a blanket with a hot cup of cocoa as I sat down to give a statement to Deacon. Since getting picked up neither Deacon nor Jack had left me alone for so much as a minute. Lizzy arrived shortly after the news had traveled along the grapevine.

"Do you mind if we talk one to one?" Deacon said to me. He eyed Jack across the table in the small interview room.

Jack bristled. "I'm her lawyer. She's well within her rights to have one present with her."

"That decision falls on Chelsea." Deacon glared at Jack.

"Well if you let her open her mouth maybe she might—"

"Gentlemen, gentlemen! Calm down please!"

At my insistence both men went quiet. The image of strutting peacocks came to mind. Not only were they both acting completely out of character, but I felt darn uncomfortable stuck in the middle of their testosterone throwdown.

It was only several hours later that I finally managed to make it back to Lizzy's loft, and even then, Deacon had insisted a unit would be placed outside 'just to make sure'. Lizzy and I were too wired to sleep when we got in, so we just sat in her kitchen eating cookies and going over the strange evening.

"Intuition," Lizzy said. She was flipping through the witch's digest she had summoned a week earlier. "I summoned this when I couldn't sleep. I was trying to figure out how you teach an adult witch magic. This issue was the one that came to me."

"So?"

"So..." She turned the book around and opened it to its middle page. "Look at the featured article. It's a guide for magical pest control. *Problems with dark-fairies? Soak five cups of Sleeping Reaper mushroom in a bowl of water and leave the drained solution out overnight. These troublesome critters can't resist the draught, and it's strong enough to kill a fully-grown man!*'"

"Your intuition was trying to lead you to the answer," I said.

"It was under our noses the whole time!"

Some point after that we managed to find sleep. In the days

following I kept myself busy by listening to my intuition when I could, learning the basics of starter magic and learning as many witch runes as I possibly could.

I even managed to find time to have dinner with Jack and Deacon. Separately of course. And it was just dinner. Nothing more. Nothing less.

In my mind I had planned on staying on the island for two weeks, and when my original departure day flew by, I found that I didn't really notice. I was far too busy catching up on a lifetime of magical education and trying to dip my toes into an ocean that was unlike anything I had ever seen before in my life. There were so many new questions on my mind every day that I had to start writing stuff down just to keep track.

If I was going to really live on the island full time, then I would have to start thinking about money again and how I was going to fund a life here. The little cash in Griselda's estate was enough to keep me going for now, but I had to look forward to the future and make a plan.

I next saw Mary Malkin again when I was up at the house on Cherry Road. Artemis was busy doing backflips in the front yard because my new bed had just been delivered. Adam was helping me move the large box inside when Mary pulled up to the house front in a rusted old Volkswagen beetle.

She stepped out of the car and approached me. Mary was still wearing her 'Don't Hassle the Hoff!' t-shirt, but this time she also had denim dungarees and large platform heels that could have been pulled off a Spice Girl. Her long silver hair was tied up in the most intricate updo.

"You solved your thing. Now comes the next thing," she said absently.

"Oh, hey, Mary! Do you want a cup of tea?"

"Gotta figure out your power," she said, ignoring my question completely. "What charges your magic? Where does it come from? Who are you?"

"You mean my archetype?"

"No, that's easy enough." She snapped her fingers and a piece of paper appeared in her hand. "You're an odd one, Chelsea Sponks. Lots of energy surrounding you, but you're bringing things here. Big things. Lots of room on this little island, but you're gonna make it crowded."

"I don't understand…" I said as Mary came toward me. She put the paper into my hand and walked back to her beetle.

"You will soon!" she shouted back. "You will soon! Or maybe you won't, what do I care? I've done my job. Now it's time to do yours."

Without another word the bizarre witch drove off. I looked at Adam and Artemis, who were both standing on the porch looking very confused.

"She's eccentric," I said.

"I'm going to move this inside." Adam picked up the box containing my bed and carried it inside, making it look as though it weighed nothing.

"What's the note say?" Artemis said as he jumped onto a porch post. I unfolded the paper and saw a brief paragraph written in witch runes. They popped into English as soon as I set my eyes on them. The clipping was from Witch's Digest.

The Sleuth

Perhaps the rarest of all, this witch draws her magical power from curiosity itself. When there's mystery afoot you will find this witch working to her wits end to try and unravel whatever conundrum she might face. Her magic is at its strongest when a question is burning in her ear and should there be a dull moment, she might find it doesn't last long. The Sleuth is a magnet for all things unusual. Trouble follows the Sleuth, and Sleuths follow trouble.

"Well?" Artemis said. "What's it say?"

I folded the clipping up and slipped it into my pocket. I looked at Artemis and scratched his head. "It looks like I might be staying here a while kitty. But we're going to have to do something about this house."

I walked back inside, and Artemis followed me. A familiar black specter was waiting for me in the hall. It was the ghost of the pirate, Old Mad John, he rushed forward and screamed at me.

"Get out!" he said. "Hang on the mast!"

Without thinking I flicked my hand up and yelled, "Nitras!" Flame burst from my fingers and Old Mad John evaporated into cloud before he could reach me.

"Nice!" Artemis said. "Keep it up and I'll soon be out of a job."

"Eh, you can stay. You're better at catching mice than me anyway."

"You're not going to tell me what was on the paper, are you?" he grumbled as we walked up the stairs.

"What's wrong with a little bit of mystery, Artemis? Sometimes it's more fun leaving things to the imagination."

"Um, hello, did you ever hear about curiosity killing the cat?"

"I think Adam will get there before curiosity does, if you keep winding him up the way you are."

As if on cue, Adam's voice came booming from the top landing.

"Why are there cat-sized bite marks in my bologna sandwich!? I'm gonna kill that rat!"

"Gotta go!" Artemis squeaked and he bolted down the stairs. Adam quickly thundered down after him.

"Bed's upstairs. I'll help you build it as soon as I wring that cat's neck!"

The giant groundskeeper was out the front door a moment later and I could hear Artemis wailing with laughter in the distance.

Standing there on the stairs I felt the space of the empty house around me. It looked like this was the next chapter in my life, and as I listened to the silence, I felt something whispering in my ear. It was a quiet voice, one I suspected that had been there all my life, but I was only just hearing it now for the first time. There were only two words, and they were very simple. I found myself whispering them back to the walls.

"I'm home."

Click here to get book 2 'A Witch Before the Storm' available now.

THANKS FOR READING

Thanks for reading, I hope you enjoyed the book. It would really help me out if you could leave an honest review with your thoughts and rating on Amazon. Every bit of feedback helps!

MAILING LIST

Want to be notified when I release my latest book? Join my mailing list. It's for new releases only. No spam.

http://eepurl.com/gIHYJj

www.ingramcontent.com/pod-product-compliance
Lightning Source LLC
Chambersburg PA
CBHW020529160726
47992CB00005BA/2313